The horse galloped into the yard. O'Fallon dropped the reins as he jumped from the horse and kicked open the door.

Hansen held a cocked gun on a bloodied man, aimed at his kneecap. O'Fallon grabbed Hansen's throat and gun hand and pulled him through the door into the night. The gun went off harmlessly. O'Fallon pried it from the other man's grasp and tossed it into the weeds.

Hansen turned, furious.

"I don't know who the hell you are, but you've bit yourself off a passel of trouble—"

O'Fallon backhanded Hansen's face. His head snapped back, and he looked at O'Fallon in wide-eyed surprise.

"You! What are you doing here?" He rubbed his cheek.

"I'm going to kill you, you son of a bitch," O'Fallon replied.

Something in O'Fallon's face hinted of madness, and for the first time in years Hansen became worried.

A COLD, DARK TRAIL

Frank Watson

FAWCETT GOLD MEDAL • NEW YORK

Sale of this book without a front cover may be unauthorized. If this book is coverless, it may have been reported to the publisher as "unsold or destroyed" and neither the author nor the publisher may have received payment for it.

A Fawcett Gold Medal Book
Published by Ballantine Books
Copyright © 1991 by Frank Watson

All rights reserved under International and Pan-American Copyright Conventions. Published in the United States by Ballantine Books, a division of Random House, Inc., New York, and simultaneously in Canada by Random House of Canada Limited, Toronto.

Library of Congress Catalog Card Number: 91-91986

ISBN 0-449-14766-5

Manufactured in the United States of America

First Edition: October 1991

Prologue

St. Louis, Missouri
March 1866

Every step brought new agony. Sean O'Fallon clenched his fists and tried not to think about the pain in his leg.

Sean's pace was now little more than a jog. His wounded leg hit the semifrozen ground heavily with a slow, rhythmic thud that each time sent a new jolt through his body. He would never again be able to run for miles through the mountains as he had before the war, but at least he could cover considerable ground at a steady pace. Ten months before, the doctors had said he would never walk again, but Sean had known better. His stubbornness had proven them wrong.

Today, for the first time, he had made it past the downtown business district to the river bluffs and back. Though it was only a small victory, and his leg was still weak, Sean had met the goal he had set for himself. He could wait no longer. Tomorrow, he would start the long journey home, pain or no pain.

The chilly breeze carried the distant, muddy scent of the Mississippi and the sharper smell of burning coal from the factories. It made the young man ache even more for the clean forest smells of his home in the Cumberland Mountains of Tennessee and the warmth of a wife he had not seen in over two years.

Sean slowed his pace as he entered the woods. He walked steadily, firmly, as long shadows fell on the rapidly freezing ground. He turned, taking a side path through the trees and beyond. Suddenly the Malcolm Home appeared before him, reflecting an orange tint from the setting sun. Some of the residents were still walking carefully under the bare trees.

The W. F. Malcolm Home had been a temporary hospital during the war and was now serving as a convalescent home under the direction of a volunteer group, Friends of the Union Veterans. A walk led from the side street to the door. Porches sat on the first and second stories.

Sean noticed Diane Blair and Dr. Jenkins on the first-floor porch where he had to pass. The young man continued his steady pace, though his leg was already becoming stiff. He had made up his mind, and he did not want a scene on the final night of his stay at the Malcolm House. Diane had been good to him. She had been good company and Sean owed much of his recovery to her tender caring. He would miss her, but he missed his wife in Tennessee more, and now it was time to go home.

"You've been gone a long time," Diane said, almost before Sean had gotten within hearing distance. "We were getting worried about you."

She had a pretty smile, and there was concern in her eyes.

"I started early, before the sun was up," Sean answered. "I wanted to cover a lot of ground today. I made it to the river, around the edge of the city, and back."

"I wish you wouldn't push yourself so hard. You're not ready for those hills."

"She's right, you know," Jenkins added. He was now sitting on the porch bannister. "You push that leg too far and you might hurt it beyond repair. I recommend rest."

"And you know so much. You were one of the doctors that said I would never walk again. You said I would be a cripple for the rest of my life. You recommended bed rest and fought me every step of the way when I started my own walking program. Had I listened to you, I would have remained a cripple."

"Miracles do happen," Jenkins said. "That is why I've followed your case so closely. There is still much we don't understand about medical science. You're an interesting case."

Sean stepped onto the wooden porch. Diane reached out, touched his arm, and said, "Please, Sean, take better care of yourself."

Jenkins crossed his arms, watching the man and woman with interest, but said nothing.

Sean waited patiently, looking out to the green yard, but Jenkins made no effort to move from his seat. Sean finally said, "Diane, could I talk to you for a few minutes? Alone?"

She followed the young man into the front room, which was filled with resting veterans, up the stairs, and into his room. For once, the room was empty in spite of the cots lined up along the walls.

"What is it?"

"I wanted you to know. I'm leaving tomorrow."

She sat down heavily on Sean's cot.

"But you can't. You're not well enough. You heard what the doctor said. . . ."

"I can't wait any longer. I've been gone from home too long. It's been almost three years without any word, without any answers to my letters. I'm going home."

"Sean—"

"Wait, before you say anything else. I'm grateful for what you've done for me, and I don't know any other way to say it. If not for your care, I might very well now be dead, or a cripple. You're a very special woman. I wish you happiness. I wish I could show you my appreciation in some way. . . ."

"You know what I would like."

"And you know that is the one thing I can't give you. You've always known I was married, and that I would eventually be going home."

Diane wet her lips, and stood. She said, "But you were married less than a week when you went to war. Your wife hasn't answered your letters in all the years you've been away. How can you know—"

Sean's look was hard, and her comment was stopped in

midsentence. She thought for a second, then continued, "How do you plan to get home?"

"Walk. That's what I've been working for these past months."

"What will you do for money?"

He reached into his pocket, pulled out three silver coins.

"It's not much, but it will do."

Diane didn't want to give up. She said, "Even if you can make the journey, how do you expect to survive? The country is still filled with bushwhackers. The papers are filled with stories about Quantrill, Bloody Bill Anderson, Winston Culver. They've robbed banks, shot sheriffs' deputies, attacked farmhouses, killing entire families. You're just one man. You won't be safe against those murdering gangs. Stay with me. You'll be safe here."

Sean painfully crouched down, reached under the bed, and pulled out a cardboard box. He lifted the lid, removed a Remington .44 caliber New Model revolver and a box of cartridges.

"Another legacy of the war," he said. "I was a good hand with a gun before the war and during the war. Back home, I used an old Kentucky rifle, but I learned to do fairly well with the Remington. A bum leg may slow me down, but it doesn't make me helpless. I'll be fine."

Diane watched Sean place the revolver on the bed.

"Nothing I can do or say will change your mind."

"No."

She suddenly reached out and hugged Sean. For the first time, he responded. He placed his arms around the woman and let her rest her head on his shoulder.

"Your wife is a very lucky woman," she whispered. Then, as if nothing had happened, she stepped back. "I won't be here tomorrow when you leave. I hope you understand."

"Yes. I understand."

Diane turned and walked from the room. For long minutes, the silence in the pale room was broken only by the sounds of cartridges being placed in the chambers of the revolver.

Chapter 1

On the Indian Territory Border
September 1869

The explosion shattered the quiet afternoon air. A shower of dirt, rocks, and wood chips floated through the sunlight and settled on Sean O'Fallon and Norman Grady, who were kneeling safely behind a small rock outcropping.

When the smoke and dust drifted away on the autumn breeze, the two men stood and walked to the shallow depression in the field. Pieces of root in the ground and larger chunks of wood around the edge were all that remained of the stump. Grady bent over the hole as if to examine it closer and said, "Fine job. Excellent job. It's a wonder how you know exactly how much powder to use and where to place it. Where'd you pick up that skill without getting yourself blown up first?"

O'Fallon removed his Stetson and knocked off the wood chips. "In the army," he said. "During the war. I knew pretty much about powder and such before I went in, and they kind of built on it. Sometimes what I learned comes in handy."

Grady kicked at the dirt and chips with his foot and answered absently, "Yeah, I suppose some good things came out of the war."

"Mighty few."

"Yeah, I guess so." Grady was slightly overweight with a red face beneath his narrow-brimmed hat. He mopped his face with a handkerchief and walked to the next stump, which had roots growing into the ground beneath a protruding rock. "At this rate, we'll have most of the field cleared in another day, which is perfect. We're expecting the first families to arrive within the next few weeks. I don't guess you came across any wagons headed in this direction? You'd have made better time since all you're leading is a packhorse."

O'Fallon thought Grady tended to talk before he had much to say, but that suited O'Fallon well enough. O'Fallon answered politely, "No, I came up from the southwest, so our paths wouldn't cross."

"Well, they'll be here soon, and when they arrive, their land will be ready for them and they can start building."

"Kind of late in the year to start, isn't it?"

"Well, maybe. But rumor has it that the railroad may build through here, and the Eastern investor financing this project wants us to be ready for it."

"It seems like everybody these days are looking for the railroads to build through their backyards and make their fortunes. A lot of would-be cities have been left out in the cold when the railroad passed them by."

"That's true in some cases. But even if the railroad doesn't build exactly through this point, we'll still be sitting pretty. And do you know why?" Grady pointed toward the west. "Look over there."

O'Fallon saw only tree-covered hills stretching toward the horizon.

"That's Indian Territory," Grady said. "Right now, that part of the country is still off-limits to the white man. That will change. There's a lot of good land in there. Good cattle country. Good farm country. Right now the Cherokees are keeping the land to themselves. But mark my words: that whole area will be opened up within the next few years. Even if it is not *legally* opened during that time, a steady stream of people will still be crossing the border. And when the crowds start coming, I'll be ready for them, me and my family. Even though they may have equipped themselves back in St. Louis or St. Joseph or wherever, they'll still have to buy supplies from somebody, and I'll be waiting for them.

Oh, this doesn't look like much now—just my store, my house, and a few outbuildings—but the town will grow fast. Think I'll call it Grady's Crossing."

O'Fallon had to admit that the location was good. O'Fallon had been following one of the trails toward Indian Territory when he came upon Grady's store and the partially cleared land. He had been surprised when he rode up the day before, hitched his horse and packhorse to the post in front of the store, and walked into the building to be greeted by Grady like an old friend. He was a talker, and any stranger would have suited Grady just fine.

As they talked, Grady explained his dilemma. He was a businessman, not a workingman, and had trouble enough cutting down trees, much less removing the stumps. Yet, the Eastern capitalist financing the project expected quick results, including clearing the land and getting much of the construction completed by the first snow. O'Fallon noted the kegs of blasting powder in the store and offered his services. Grady jumped at the chance. O'Fallon was looking for information more than work, but he figured that Grady might help him obtain what he really wanted.

"Yes, sir, there are fortunes to be made," Grady said. "Just across the border are acres and acres of land. Thousands of acres of land. And that's what people want. That's what people need. It's our destiny to expand to the West, to build up the empty land, to bring civilization. And you know what else?" Grady lowered his voice. "There are plenty of men back East with vision and with the capital to spend—like the one that's staked me. If you can hitch up to a man like that, your fortune is made."

"What about the Indians? I thought that by law the land is theirs."

"What about them? They're just Indians, and when the people start pushing across the border, the Indians will just have to go elsewhere." Grady walked over and kicked the stump near the rock. "This one looks kind of tricky."

"No problem." O'Fallon glanced up at the sun. A dark gray cloud was moving rapidly and cast a brief shadow on the ground. "It may take a little more powder, but we'll have this patch cleared by evening, before the thunderstorm hits."

O'Fallon lifted one of the powder kegs to his shoulder and walked over to the stump. He took the shovel and quickly dug another hole, this one a little deeper. He pulled the cork from the keg and poured the gray-black powder into the depression. Grady watched, mopping his face, as O'Fallon prepared the powder, then measured and inserted the proper length of fuse.

"This should give us plenty of time to get out of the way," O'Fallon said. "And even if we didn't, I doubt if we would be hurt. The explosion should blow the stump and rocks away from us, if I figure right."

"If you figure right?"

O'Fallon grinned slightly.

"Oh, don't worry. I haven't blown up very many of my employers. So why start now?"

"Yes. Oh, yes."

"Hell with that. Why not blow up the bastard when you have the chance. While you're at it, blow up that damned store, as well." The new voice was coarse and slurred. It came from behind O'Fallon and to his left.

Grady said harshly, "Turk, what are you doing here? I told you we didn't want you around."

"So you say, but you sell your whiskey fast enough. Besides, I wanted to experience the so-called 'pleasures of civilization' that you are always carrying on about."

Turk had obviously been drinking, even though it was still early afternoon. O'Fallon had spotted Turk earlier, and had watched the man skulk around the clearing for the greater part of an hour, drinking his whiskey from a jug, building up the courage to make his presence known.

"I don't want you around me or my family," Grady said. "Get out of here."

O'Fallon watched as Grady's hands moved nervously and Turk's eyes remained hard. O'Fallon stood, walked to the rock outcropping that had served as protection from the explosions, and pulled out his pipe and tobacco. He noted

Turk's faded checkered shirt, the old revolver in a holster around his hips, and the jug in his left hand.

"You go to hell," Turk said, taking a step toward Grady. "You think I give a damn about what you want? It was just fine before you came along, but now a man doesn't even have room to piss. Nobody needs you. Nobody wants you. *You* just get out of here." Turk glanced at O'Fallon, who was now calmly smoking his pipe. "And take your damned greenhorn friend with you. I want *everybody* out."

Grady nervously looked around him. He stepped back as Turk moved closer.

"Last time you hit me from the rear, and I should have killed you then," Turk said. "I don't like cowards, but now I'm facing you, and I'm going to teach you and this greenie a thing or two."

Turk reached for his gun, but he suddenly found himself staring at a rifle in O'Fallon's hands.

"Don't try it, Turk," O'Fallon said.

Turk blinked a few times in disbelief.

"Where'd that come from?"

"Just because I'm not wearing a gun doesn't mean I'm green. I'm a fairly good shot, and at this distance I couldn't miss. I don't want to hurt you. Just remove your hand from the gun, take your whiskey, and go home."

The other man hesitated, but when O'Fallon refused to move the aim of the gun from his stomach, Turk growled, spit, and stomped back toward the store. Only after Turk had turned the corner and was out of sight did O'Fallon again place his rifle behind the rock outcropping.

O'Fallon puffed on his pipe and suggested, "Maybe you should go after him to make sure he leaves?"

"Maybe." But instead, Grady sat down on the rock next to O'Fallon and said, "Turk talks big, but most of the time he keeps to himself, except when he's drinking. He lives up in the hills, somewhere, in the territory. He knows these hills, lives off some trapping and trading with the Indians. I almost feel sorry for old Turk. He and the Indians had these hills to themselves for a long time, and that's all changing.

But that's his problem, not mine. He did try to buffalo me once, but I managed to handle him. I don't trust him, and I don't want him around my family. Maybe he won't come back."

O'Fallon calmly smoked his pipe, but all the while scanned the woods around the clearing to make sure Turk did not return. In spite of all his talk, Grady still had not voluntarily provided the information that most interested O'Fallon. He decided to use this break to prime the pump a little more.

"This is a pretty good location, at that," O'Fallon said, stretching out his long legs. "I guess most of those going into the territory pass through here, which means you pretty well know everybody who has entered the territory recently or who operates in the territory. Maybe you could tell me about a man I'm looking for?"

"Could be. What's the name?"

"Winston Culver." Grady frowned. O'Fallon continued in a neutral voice, "During the war he led a group of bushwhackers that were active in Tennessee, Kentucky, Missouri. They covered a lot of ground. I've been looking for him for several years now, without any luck. I still hear a lot of talk. I follow the rumors, but I can never quite catch up to him. Now I hear he's active in Indian Territory."

"I've heard the name," Grady said. "But it was from back East, mainly during the war. I don't know of him being anywhere in these parts." He brushed some dust off the rock. "How do you tie in to Culver?"

"Let's just say I owe him a long-standing debt."

"Hmph."

"Maybe he's using a different name. He's about six feet tall, gray eyes, gray hair, even though he's not too old."

"He hasn't passed through here that I know about. I haven't heard of him coming through. And I don't remember seeing anybody of that description."

So he had been following another false lead. O'Fallon tapped his pipe lightly on the rock to shake out the ashes.

"Time to get back to work," he said. "You wait here."

O'Fallon lit the fuse and moved quickly back to safety.

A COLD, DARK TRAIL

The two men sat with backs against the rock as the fuse sparked and hissed. Suddenly, a high-pitched yell cut through the afternoon air.

"Daddy! Daddy! Daddy!"

O'Fallon pushed himself up, looked over the rock. Grady's four-year-old son was running, stumbling. His path was taking him right to the stump where the fuse was burning rapidly toward the powder.

Grady said, "Joe! What the hell is he doing—"

O'Fallon jumped to his feet and leaped over the rock, but he landed slightly crooked, bending his leg. Ignoring the pain that suddenly shot through him, he started across the clearing. Behind him, he could hear Grady yelling at his son. O'Fallon saw that Joe was half crying, half yelling, and was on the wrong side of the blast—the direction in which most of the force would hit.

O'Fallon's leg felt like it was on fire, but he did not slow down. He had no family, and would probably never have a family, and it somehow made getting Joe to safety seem all the more important. He glanced at the fuse, but it was now too short to see.

A half-dozen yards remained between Joe and O'Fallon, who was quickly closing the distance.

The boy stumbled only a few feet from the stump. O'Fallon made a flying leap. He scooped up the boy in his arms, fell, and tumbled. O'Fallon stood, set his good leg solidly to the ground, then dived behind one of the remaining stumps in the field.

The explosion sent rock chips in all directions. O'Fallon used his body to shield the boy, but the main force of the blast missed them.

O'Fallon placed the boy against the stump and started to examine him. He was crying and coughing when Grady made it through the smoke and dust. Joe was trying not to cry. He reached out to Grady and said, "Daddy!"

"Joe, I told you not to come out here when we're working. I should whip you for disobeying me."

"But Daddy! The nasty man hit Mommy! That dirty man

you sold the jugs to came back and took Mr. O'Fallon's horse and packs. Mommy took your shotgun to him, but he pushed her down and locked me in the back room. I climbed out the window!"

Grady grabbed his son and started to run across the field. O'Fallon retrieved his rifle and followed Grady back to the store. They met Mrs. Grady near the building.

"You all right?" Grady's voice was concerned, scared. "What the hell happened? Are you hurt?"

O'Fallon noted the small bruise on the woman's face, but decided she was not seriously hurt. He left the family to handle his own business. His sorrel remained in the pole corral behind the store, but the packhorse was gone. The packs he had stacked in the stables were gone, but his saddle remained untouched. He continued his search of the area.

Turk had made no attempt to cover his tracks around the building. He apparently thought he had the superior woodsman's skills and could lose himself in the trees. Or maybe he thought that O'Fallon would not even try to follow? O'Fallon knew Turk would probably make a halfhearted attempt to cover his trail once he hit the woods.

O'Fallon walked around the building, then entered through the front door, placing the saddle on the front step. Grady was tending to his wife.

"You're right, Mr. O'Fallon. I should have followed and made sure he left."

"Then he might have pulled a gun and you'd be dead."

After a few moments of awkward silence, Grady's wife said, "I understand you saved our son. I want to thank you."

"I'm sorry about your things being stolen," Grady said. "I mean, you were good enough to help me out, and now this had to happen. Maybe there is something I can do? I can't replace your entire stock, but maybe I could—"

"What do you plan to do about your wife?"

The question seemed to puzzle Grady.

"I mean, are you going after Turk?"

"What would be the use? Nobody knows where he lives. He knows this part of the country, and will already have vanished. Even if we could find him, he would ambush us easily. It'd be suicide to go after him. No, I'm leaving well enough alone."

"Yes, I guess you were lucky at that. He could have killed your wife and son." O'Fallon paused, then continued, "I'm going to quit on you early. I know I promised to clear the whole field, but under the circumstances I think I had better move on."

Grady pulled out some money and placed it on the table.

"Go ahead and take your full wages. You earned it."

O'Fallon set his saddlebags by the bills.

"I need a couple of boxes of shells, some coffee, flour, and tobacco. Take what I owe you out of my pay."

Joe was looking up at O'Fallon with wide eyes.

"Joe, would you and your mother go get my horse and bring it around so I can saddle it up?"

The boy ran out, followed by Mrs. Grady.

"What about next time?" O'Fallon asked.

Grady was pulling supplies from the shelves and placing them on the table near the saddlebags. He said, "What do you mean?"

"Think about what you're doing," O'Fallon continued. "You're a good man, I think, trying to do the best you can for your family. But this is not like the East, where you have laws and police to enforce them. Out here, you stand on your own or die. You underestimated Turk. He's a dangerous man, but there are many out here who are far worse. I've known men who would have raped your wife, then shot her and the boy, and not give any of it a second thought. You think about what you have—a wife and a family. And think about if you want to risk it all for a fortune that may or may not ever materialize."

"Where will you be going next?" Grady asked, strangely quiet.

"To get back my horse and goods. I'm going after Turk."

"You won't stand a chance. How can you expect to find anybody in the wilderness of the Indian Territory?"

"I'll find him."

Chapter 2

Jack Hansen at first thought the rifle shot was thunder from the dark, low-hanging clouds that had been following him since he entered the Indian Territory. His big, black stallion jumped at the sound and Hansen's breath whistled sharply through his teeth.

Hansen was afraid of no man, but lightning and fire were different matters. He had seen one man, who had not taken shelter soon enough, in an instant burned beyond recognition by a lightning bolt. He knew all too well how quickly death could come to a man without protection from the elements, and he had no plans to die this night.

What he needed now was some shelter.

The late summer storm had been building for most of the afternoon. Hansen was now on relatively high ground, as he had been for the past several miles, but still no shelter was in sight.

Hansen anxiously scanned the horizon while the big stallion pawed the ground.

The smell of rain was in the air. The clouds grew darker by the minute. He was no woodsman, but he knew the storm would hit soon and hard. He couldn't face a night of thunder and lightning without protection, but where could he go? All he had seen for miles were thickets, fields, gullies, and creeks. None of them provided any real safety. This stretch of the territory was thinly populated, and Hansen was new to the area. He had no idea where to even start looking for shelter.

The stallion jumped sharply as wind-blown bushes brushed against it. Hansen cursed.

Another shot rang out from beyond the ridge in front of Hansen. This shot was sharper, clearer, from a handgun of some sort. A second and third shot quickly followed from the same gun.

A rifle shot, as loud as thunder, answered the handgun fire.

Hansen smiled, relieved. The sound that had spooked his horse had not been thunder. Instead, it was a gunshot from a shoot-out, less than a mile away. This kind of trouble Hansen could understand, handle, even welcome. A gunfight meant there would be a loser, and a winner, and something worth winning. Shelter. Money. Food. Maybe even a woman! It had been quite a few miles since his last woman, and he was ready for another.

He thought about the two whores he had left behind in New Hope, just a few days before, and almost laughed out loud. They had been enough to keep him satisfied for a while, but already his need was strong again. A woman would suit him just fine! Still, his main concern now was protection from the storm.

More shots were suddenly exchanged. Three more handgun shots for one rifle shot. Hansen grinned wolfishly as he urged his stallion forward. He dismounted before he reached the crest of the hill, and loosely wrapped the stallion's reins around a sapling.

Slowly, carefully, Hansen started up the slight incline. He was confident he could not be seen, but there was no use taking chances. It was his way to watch, to wait, and then to strike like a rattlesnake, Hansen thought proudly. In fact, when he had been riding with Culver's Raiders during the war, it had been Hansen who came up with the idea of using the rattlesnake as the symbol of the group on their flag. He had personally smeared the rattlesnake sign on many of the walls of houses and the headboards of beds that had seen his—and Culver's—conquests.

Even now, the memory of those women sent a familiar tingle through Hansen.

The thoughts made his excitement even greater, and he then decided that finding another woman was his next priority after the storm had passed. He figured he could mix in a little pleasure with his assignment.

The trip so far had been dry and dusty, but now the ground seemed damp even though the rain had not yet started. The growing wind pushed against Hansen's Stetson. The hat was new, as were all his clothes. He had purchased them in New Hope before starting on this job. They were already covered with dust and soaked with sweat, but that did not hide the expensive cut and material. Hansen believed that expensive clothes gave him a distinguished look. The entire outfit was black.

His boots were even fancier than his clothes. The leather had been buffed to a high gloss. They would have cost an average cowboy half his wages for a year, but had barely made a dent in Hansen's expense account.

Hansen pulled the Smith & Wesson revolver from his left holster as he neared the top of the hill. The holster, like the boots, was of smooth leather, finely finished and well oiled. His guns were the latest style and type, using metal cartridges. They were easier to load, could be drawn quickly, and were accurate, especially at close ranges. He cleaned and oiled them almost religiously.

The gunfighter removed his hat, dropped to his stomach, and crawled up the last several feet of the hillside. The grass was still green, though starting to turn brown. Late summer flowers and colored bushes hid the fight taking place in the hollow below. The stallion neighed softly, but Hansen figured the sound would be lost in the wind.

Hansen cautiously pushed to one side a small sassafras bush that had turned prematurely red. The scent from the bruised leaves mixed with the damp earthen smell. The other side of the hill dropped gradually toward a small, sagging log house and attached corral.

Shelter!

The log structures looked as if they were about to fall, but they would meet his needs. Anything was better than being exposed to the rain and lightning.

A fully loaded packhorse was in the corral.

A grizzled man in a faded checkered shirt was hiding behind the ramshackle log house. He was holding a handgun, looking fearfully toward a steep, wooded hill to Hansen's right.

The gunfighter figured that the man had been surprised shortly after his arrival, before he could unpack the horse in the corral. His attacker was now safely under cover of the heavy woods. Hansen smiled, and silently congratulated the unseen man in the woods for setting such a successful trap. It seemed to be a good ambush—one such as Hansen himself might have set.

The trapped man was clumsily trying to reload his revolver. He stretched his neck, then started to crawl. A rifle fired from the woods. The bullet kicked up dirt and dust just inches from the head of the red-shirted figure, who quickly scurried back to his hiding place.

Hansen could not see the man in the woods, but from the brief rifle flash believed he knew the attacker's exact location. The shot had come from behind a wide tree next to a pile of rocks. It was a good location, providing a hidden view of the hollow.

Hansen, however, believed his vantage point to be better. It allowed him to observe the entire scene playing out before him without being seen in return, which gave him the edge. He felt a sudden surge of power, as if the men shooting at each other in front of him were doing so strictly for his entertainment, as if he were some kind of god.

Lightning flashed in the distance, making Hansen jump, but also reinforcing the image in his mind. He liked this chain of thought, and allowed it to grow. After all, wasn't he a kind of god? He took what he wanted. He did what he wanted. He made others do his bidding. And then there were the women! So many women had looked upon him with adoring eyes as he wore them down, made them scream, made them thank him for loving them. It was only natural that the name of Jack Hansen would inspire fear and awe. It was only natural to take what was his by right. Some would never understand this truth. Hansen, however, could take a life as easily as a woman, and enjoy that as well.

The pitiful, trapped man looked warily around him, then toward a smaller patch of woods to his rear. Hansen knew what the other man was thinking:

I am trapped.

I have no hope for escape.

I am a dead man.

It was a game Hansen sometimes played with his own victims: trying to determine their thoughts just before killing them.

Hansen had no sympathy for the trapped man. He had been a fool for allowing himself to be trapped. He was weak, and was now suffering the consequences of his foolishness. The fool deserved to die, as far as Hansen was concerned.

He had personally killed men for lesser reason.

Hansen silently urged the unseen man in the woods to make his move, to bring the action to its bloody close. He was suddenly in a better mood at the anticipation of seeing a good kill.

A sudden clap of thunder sounded overhead and a large raindrop hit Hansen's bare head. He cursed silently, his good mood gone as quickly as it had come. He hoped the two fighters would end the battle soon, before the storm hit.

Instead, the woods and hollow grew quiet. The sounds of distant rain starting to fall heavily could be clearly heard.

"Get on with it," Hansen growled.

Another raindrop fell. The lightning grew closer. The smell of rain was stronger.

Finally, the man behind the cabin decided to make his escape under the cover of the late twilight. He tried to remain hidden in the lengthening shadows—a deeper black among shades of black—as he crawled toward the trees. Hansen squinted, trying to keep the figure in view.

Hansen waited for a shot from the woods, but none came. Damn! Was the hunter going to let his prey get away? Hansen thought for a moment that he might have to kill the grizzled man himself.

Encouraged by the lack of shooting, the man on the ground stood and started to run.

Mistake, Hansen thought. You fool. You can't possibly escape that way.

Still, no shot came from the wooded hill, so the figure ran even faster. Hansen lifted his own gun, and was aiming, when the running man was stopped in midstride by a strong voice in front of him. So the hunter had also made his move, effectively cutting off even this slight chance of escape!

"Good," Hansen muttered. "A good move."

The mouth of the red-shirted man flew open, but no words came out.

The voice in the woods repeated, "Stop, and drop your gun. I don't want to kill you, Turk."

The trapped man stared vacantly into the darkness. Hansen frowned. What was going on? The prey was caught neatly in the open, so why delay the killing?

"I don't want to kill you, Turk. This is Sean O'Fallon, the man you stole that horse from back at Grady's store. Just put down your gun, and I'll take my horse and packs and be gone."

The trapped man looked left and right, right and left, stepped backward into deeper shadow.

"You can't escape. You should know that by now. Grady's wife wasn't seriously hurt, and it's not my problem. I just want my goods back and I'll be on my way. Don't make me kill you."

Shoot, fool! Hansen thought. Don't give him a chance to escape!

Still, the man hidden in the woods did not shoot. Hansen spit in disgust. This man was as big of a fool as the trapped one! Only a weakling ever gave a trapped man a chance to escape.

It was now dark enough that Hansen could no longer see the trapped man's face. Hansen did see the panicky way the man slowly raised his revolver.

Turk fired once. His aim was unsteady, and the bullet did not come close to its target.

A burst of flame shot out from the woods. Turk spun backward. He turned and fired a series of shots into the woods.

A second shot flashed from the woods and a second bright red spot appeared on the front of the faint red of the shirt.

The gun dropped from the man's hand. He took one last step forward, coughed once, then fell dully to the ground.

The show was over, but Hansen decided to remain quiet.

For long minutes, the only sounds were the wind, the rain now falling more steadily, the rolling thunder moving closer. The man on the ground did not move even as the water started to pool around him. The darkness grew and the rain dripped down the back of Hansen's neck.

Finally, the winner of the fight made his appearance. He was a young man, apparently in his early twenties, walking with a very slight limp, carrying a repeating rifle in his hand. He calmly stepped over to the dead man, kicked the revolver out of reach, used his foot to roll the body over. The shirt was now soaked, whether from blood or from rain Hansen could not tell.

The man with the rifle bent over, placed his fingers on the dead man's neck to check for a pulse. Only when he found none did he turn his attention elsewhere.

He did not seem to be aware of Hansen's presence. The young man looked around him, and at one point seemed to look toward and through Hansen, but never directly at him.

The gunfighter nodded, thinking he already knew all there was to know about the victor of the fight just played out before him. The man had called himself O'Fallon. Hansen did not know the name. O'Fallon was apparently cautious and smart, but neither cautious enough nor smart enough. He had overlooked Hansen's presence and had apparently not even thought to scout the area for other potential enemies.

He won't live long that way, Hansen thought. Had he wanted to, Hansen could have easily picked off the other man with a single shot. In spite of the rain, however, Hansen was feeling generous. He had just witnessed a good show and was willing to let the young man keep his life and possibly most of his winnings.

Below, O'Fallon kept an easy grasp on the rifle as he walked to the corral. He soothed the uneasy pack animal in familiar terms and loosened the straps.

Hansen decided he had waited long enough. He was soaked, muddy, and ready to relax in the dry cabin. He edged backward, placed the hat firmly on his head, stepped back into the saddle. He nudged the stallion over the hillcrest to join the other man at the cabin.

If the younger man cooperated, he would live to see another day. And if he would not cooperate? Well, then, victories could sometimes be short-lived.

Sean O'Fallon knew he was being watched.

The third man had apparently considered himself well hidden by some small bushes on a hill overlooking the hollow. O'Fallon, however, had heard the soft neigh of a strange horse in the wind and quickly noticed the movement of the sassafras bush against the wind. The sound and movement were slight and would have been missed by most men. O'Fallon, however, had grown up in the Cumberland Mountains of Tennessee, where noticing such details was the difference between having food on the table or going hungry.

O'Fallon had waited with the patience of a natural hunter until he could finally make out the shadowy outline of the stranger. Who was the third man? What did he want? Was it only common sense holding him back until the fight was over? Or was he perhaps looking for something more?

As the rain approached, O'Fallon had considered the situation. The stranger may have thought himself smart, but he had missed a better hiding place just a few hundred feet to his left. There, a rock outcropping formed a natural, dry protection. Instead, the newcomer had positioned himself on the ground, which had turned to mud as soon as the rain hit.

Turk had also thought himself smart, but had left an easy trail for a man like O'Fallon to follow. It had meandered somewhat, cut across a few creeks, but the Tennessee man had easily caught up to the trapper before evening. O'Fallon did not hate Turk for stealing his packhorse and supplies, but neither did he have any sympathy for the thief. He was tempted to shoot Turk for hitting the woman. He had felt like hitting Grady for his carelessness toward his wife and son. Many men could never experience the happiness of a family. Couldn't Grady realize just how lucky he was? O'Fallon realized, however, that it was not his problem, and decided he only wanted his horse and packs back. He did not want another killing.

Turk apparently felt safe and secure after he arrived at his cabin. O'Fallon's first warning shot corrected this notion. Turk dived for cover before he had even loosened the straps of the pack. A few more shots were exchanged, but O'Fallon's intent was more to convince Turk of his position than to kill him.

It was only a few minutes after Turk had hidden that the third man made his appearance.

O'Fallon pinned down Turk and then turned his attention to the stranger. O'Fallon silently, quickly circled around the high ground surrounding the hollow. He got close enough to the stranger to see his fancy store-bought clothes, the black Stetson, the Smith & Wesson revolvers. He moved on to the stallion and noticed the important fact that the rifle was still in its case on the horse.

The inspection took just a few seconds, and then O'Fallon had completed the circle to move behind Turk's cabin.

Then Turk made his stand, and had died.

O'Fallon waited patiently in the shadows to see what the third man would do. The storm hit, and O'Fallon knew the stranger was getting soaked and muddy in his hiding place. O'Fallon moved into the open, keeping an easy grasp on his rifle. He knew exactly where the man in black was waiting. O'Fallon was certain no man could shoot accurately with a revolver from that distance. A rifle, however, would be accurate, and if the stranger tried a sneak shot it would be the last thing he would ever do.

Rain was now coming down steadily. Lightning flashed in the sky.

O'Fallon moved to his packhorse in the corral. Details were now lost in the rain and the darkness, but O'Fallon watched the shadows. On the hill, the sassafras bush waved in a telltale fashion and then O'Fallon heard the movement of the horse through the brush. He was not surprised, therefore, to see the stranger edge over the hill on his stallion.

O'Fallon started to place his packs in the cabin, apparently indifferent to the newcomer.

"Hey! At the cabin!"

The stranger's voice was deep and abrupt.

O'Fallon glanced up at the stranger, and tried not to smile. The black clothes were wet, rumpled, and muddy. Rain was pouring off the Stetson and running down the hill in streams. The stallion slid awkwardly in the mud.

"Damned weather," the stranger said. He held his reins in one hand and his other hand was raised in the air. He swayed in the saddle as the stallion made its uneasy way down the hill. "The name is Jack Hansen."

Hansen said the words as if they should mean something. When O'Fallon didn't answer quickly enough, Hansen added, "Think I'll join you in the dry for the night."

The words were more of a statement than a question. The stranger's hand had dropped near his holster. The tone of voice irritated O'Fallon. He let it pass, though he continued to hold his rifle in an easy grasp. He neither liked nor trusted this stranger in black, but he also had no fight with him.

"I don't know how dry this place is, but help yourself," O'Fallon said.

Hansen seemed to relax, until a lightning bolt split the sky. The horse jumped. Hansen dismounted quickly and almost lost his footing in the slippery mud.

O'Fallon seemed not to notice the other man's nervousness about the lightning. Instead, he disappeared into the woods like a ghost. Another lightning bolt flashed, and thunder boomed just a fraction of a second behind it. It illuminated the scene for only an instant, but long enough to show O'Fallon leading his saddled horse out of the woods into the corral.

Three more streaks of lightning flashed, followed by cracks of thunder. Hansen flinched as he removed the saddle and tossed his own gear into the old cabin.

O'Fallon stripped the saddle and gear from his horse and followed the other man into the relative dryness of the cabin.

Chapter 3

The rain fell steadily, leaking through the old cabin roof and puddling on the floor. Thunder boomed every few seconds just outside the torn, canvas-covered window.

An hour had passed since Hansen had ridden his horse down the hill, but no reference had yet been made to the shooting he had witnessed. The only talk had been a brief exchange of names.

The cabin had little furniture. Hansen lit an old lantern, found a jug of whiskey in the corner, and staked out the lumpy cot that served as a bed. He sat with his back to the wall and his legs outstretched, taking a slow drink from time to time as he worried about the rain. Finally, his clothes started to dry and the liquor began to warm him from the inside.

O'Fallon sat on a chair next to a rough table and worked patiently. He carefully dried the outside of the packs, then removed each item, examined it, dried it, and placed it to one side. He would pause at times, tap his fingers against the table, or hold a package to the light without opening it, and then continue. Hansen noticed nothing unusual about O'Fallon's goods: flour, coffee, beans; cookware; a small shovel; a change of clothes, just as plain as the ones the young man was wearing. It was the usual variety of items required for a man who planned a long stay in the wilds. Such men were common in the West. In fact, it sometimes seemed to Hansen that the entire country was on the move. He had no complaints, however, because it provided many opportunities for a man of his talents.

Hansen quickly became bored watching O'Fallon work and turned his attention to the jug. He rolled a smoke.

As Hansen sat, smoked, and drank he realized that O'Fallon was not so much unfriendly, or hostile, as indifferent. The gunfighter was used to generating fear, or hostility; he was not used to being ignored. It made him uneasy.

Or maybe it was the lightning? The building was located on relatively low ground, but the storm seemed to be centered in the immediate area of the hollow. The smell of lightning filled the air and the floor was almost soaked from the water dripping through the roof. The old cabin, though watersoaked, could still burn quickly if a fire started.

Hansen took the last swig from the jug, then threw it to one side. He stood, nervously placed the light away from the edge of the table, and unsuccessfully looked for another jug. Finally, he examined his own saddle and gear. It was soaked, but would dry out with no problem: like his holsters and boots, he kept his tack well oiled. He glanced at O'Fallon, who continued with his own work.

Hansen placed a bridle on the table. He moved carefully, making sure the lantern was far from the edge. When O'Fallon looked up in mild curiosity, Hansen said, "Can't be too careful with fire, you know."

O'Fallon nodded. He picked up a package wrapped in brown paper, unexpectedly tossed it toward Hansen, and said, "How about some food?"

The words and the sudden movement caught Hansen by surprise. He angrily caught the package, started to slam it on the table, then stopped as he again thought about the lantern. O'Fallon looked at him calmly, without fear or surprise.

"It's bacon," O'Fallon said. "Thought I'd fry us up some."

Hansen paused, the package in his hand. He was not certain what to do next. O'Fallon was not reacting to him in the usual way. Hansen was used to men backing away from him in fear or trying to fight him. This quiet response was unexpected.

O'Fallon pulled out a clear, unmarked bottle from his bags.

"I've also got something to wash it down with," he said. "I suspect this is better than that stuff you were drinking." O'Fallon uncorked the bottle, offered it to Hansen. "Here, why not join me in a drink?"

"Damned if I will."

Hansen grabbed the full bottle, took a long swig. It was good corn whiskey, smooth, like the whiskey he used to find on his raids in Kentucky and Tennessee with Culver during and just after the war. This was better liquor than he had tasted in a long time.

"Damned good."

"Hand me that salt pork, and I'll fry us up some food. Make us both feel better."

Hansen hesitated, then said, "What the hell." He handed the package to O'Fallon and took another drink. The warmth spread from his belly. He sat back on the bed, grunted, scratched himself. The tension seemed to drain out of him and he felt a soft, warm glow.

He did not offer the bottle back to O'Fallon, who was now at the old cookstove, trying to start a fire. Raindrops fell down the flue, sizzled, released steam into the air. O'Fallon retrieved a skillet from one of his bags and soon the aroma of frying meat filled the room.

Hansen relaxed and now took the time to more closely examine the other man. He noted that O'Fallon was relatively young. His brown hair was neat. His blue eyes were dark, without emotion. A day's growth of beard darkened his strong face. Hansen begrudgingly admitted that the ladies might consider O'Fallon handsome.

His clothes were of more modest cut than Hansen's and showed much wear. His Stetson had the front turned down slightly and was faded from many hours in the sun. His boots seemed even older, with the dull sheen of many polishings.

The young man was not wearing a gun, but the Winchester

Model 1866 leaning against the wall glistened in the lantern light.

Outside, the rain was finally starting to let up. The lightning and thunder were moving to the east. Inside, Hansen was mellowed by the aroma of cooking and the warmth of good whiskey. It had been a long week's ride from New Hope into Indian Territory, and he had several more days of riding ahead of him. In comparison, this was turning out to be an enjoyable evening.

O'Fallon found some metal plates. They rattled as he placed them on the table. Hansen smiled and thought, This is the way it should always be: Jack Hansen is naturally superior, so it is only natural to be waited on!

Hansen took another drink, then cursed as he looked at the bottle. Half-empty, already!

"Goddamn."

"I have more, if you'd like," O'Fallon said, as if reading Hansen's mind. The young man forked a slice of meat to his plate and moved his chair near the stove. The rifle was within easy reach, but he did not even glance at it.

Hansen wolfed down the fatback and gravy and then filled his plate again. O'Fallon had not touched his food. He set the plate on the table and started to fill his pipe. He finally said, "I guess you're wondering about the shooting?"

The gunfighter looked up, blinked. He shook his head to clear the fog. He had almost forgotten about the shoot-out.

"Yeah. Right. Looked like you kind of lucked out, finding him unawares like that." He threw his plate to the table. "You said you have another bottle of that whiskey?"

O'Fallon retrieved the bottle from one of his packs. Hansen took care to notice which pack, for future reference. He popped the cork off the second bottle and took another drink.

"Damned fine whiskey."

"Tennessee style. I have a taste for it at times, and trade for it when I can."

Hansen nodded.

"Tennessee. Yeah, I know the place."

Normally, Hansen was tight-lipped and cautious, but the

food and good whiskey had relaxed him. Besides, this subservient stranger was obviously no threat. Sure, the young man had lucked out earlier in the evening, but the fight had been against a fool. Hansen was in a mood to brag about his conquests now that he had a captive audience.

"You from Tennessee?" O'Fallon asked.

"Naw, but I know it pretty well. I've been all over the South, all over the West. I've been everywhere there is to be, and done everything there is to do."

Hansen congratulated himself on this little speech by taking another long drink.

"I've crisscrossed the Tennessee mountains from one end to the other!" he continued. "Why, when I rode with Culver, we just about owned the state!"

Hansen watched O'Fallon for a reaction. O'Fallon's pipe, halfway to his mouth, froze for an instant. Hansen was pleased that the young man was impressed by his association with Culver. The young man placed the pipe between his teeth, bit down on it, and said softly, "You rode with Winston Culver?"

"Hell right! I was his right-hand man! We were like this!" Hansen's voice boomed and filled the damp room. He unsuccessfully tried to hold two fingers together before him.

"Everybody knows about Culver's Raiders," O'Fallon said. "I've heard him discussed from the Cumberlands to Memphis to St. Louis."

"We hit all those places, I tell you!" He lowered his voice to a more confidential, though slurred, tone. "And sometimes the pickings were a lot better in the mountains! They didn't have much gold, but they had whiskey and women!" He whooped, and whirled the bottle around his head before taking another drink. "I could sure use one of those mountain bitches right about now!" He laughed out loud, remembering. "I had my share of that, I tell you!"

O'Fallon's voice was neutral. He said, "You had quite a few women, did you?"

"Some of the bitches fought me, at first," Hansen continued. "Sometimes it took several of us to hold the gal down while the others had their fun. But when it came my turn, the women always changed their minds. They always thanked me. It was probably the first and last time they ever had a real man!"

O'Fallon puffed on his pipe. He said, "You were active in Tennessee all during the war?"

"We came and went; Tennessee was mainly toward the end. We didn't stay too long at any one place."

He took another drink, closed his eyes, and fell back against the bed. The rain dripped from the ceiling. The near-silence was broken when O'Fallon finally said, "I guess those days are over. You don't hear much about Culver's Raiders any more."

Hansen opened his eyes, suddenly wary as he remembered his current assignment. But the young man seemed only politely interested as he smoked his pipe.

"We went our separate ways," Hansen said, abruptly, but O'Fallon no longer seemed interested. He tapped his pipe on the stove, stretched out his legs, tilted his hat over his face.

"It's been a long day," he said. "You take the bed. Only the best for an ex–Culver's Raider!"

In seconds, the younger man seemed to be asleep, leaving Hansen to his thoughts. The talk had brought back memories of riding with Culver during the war. Those were the days! Taking what he wanted, when he wanted. Shelter. Food. Booze. Women. Especially the women. Some called the raiders outlaws, criminals, renegades. But a war was going on and Culver's men were hand-picked for their courage and skills. They were too valuable to waste as common soldiers! That was what Culver had drilled into his men, and they believed. And because they believed, they gave unquestioned loyalty to their leader.

Culver was not like so many small-time bushwhackers. No, he thought big, and didn't mind sharing the spoils with his men. The association with Culver remained valuable in other ways, as well. Unlike many other bushwhackers, Culver knew when to quit. He knew how to change with the times. But even though he stopped his burning and looting

A COLD, DARK TRAIL

after the war, he had remained active. He had kept his organization intact, though the activities were now relatively low-key. He continued to use the men loyal to him, paying them well for their services. This was the reason that Hansen now found himself in Indian Territory.

As Hansen leaned back on the musty bed, drinking, he again marveled at how the organization had changed. In the old days, Culver's men simply rode in, took what they wanted, and then rode on. These days, however, there were too many complications, too much secrecy, and too many people between him and Culver.

He remembered how, just a few days before, he had been waiting for the two whores at one of the best rooms at Madame Sally's, back in New Hope, and had found a single sheet of bonded paper with only a few lines handwritten in black ink slipped under his door:

Game room. New Hope Hotel. 10 P.M.

The writing was a neat, businesslike script. The note had no signature, but had a stylized rattlesnake in the lower right corner.

Hansen had played along. That night, he had showed up early, and, at the invitation of a pudgy man, had joined in a game of cards. The game had become high-stakes when Hansen pulled the pocket watch from his vest pocket, looked at it coolly.

9:55 P.M.

It was his bet.

"Well, what about it, Hansen?" the pudgy man said, his fingers nervously working the edges of the cards. "Are you in? The raise is five hundred dollars."

The table in front of Hansen was blank, and Hansen had the appearance of being cleaned out. It was all psychological, Hansen thought. He replaced his watch and slowly pulled out a dark leather wallet.

Pudgy's face went white.

"Here's your five hundred. I call."

Pudgy showed his cards: kings over threes. Hansen smiled; he had known all along Pudgy was bluffing. He turned over his own hand: three aces. He started to sweep up his winnings when Pudgy said, "I have over five thousand dollars in that pot. It cleans me out."

"Too bad."

"Give me another chance. You must—"

"Like I said. Too bad."

Hansen grinned, looked up from the table into Pudgy's eyes. The gunfighter was stopped short by what he saw. Pudgy gave the faintest glimpse of a wink, as if he were sharing a joke.

"You, sir, are a snake," Pudgy huffed mightily, but Hansen knew the reference to Culver's symbol was no accident. He felt a pang of disappointment. He had thought he was setting up Pudgy as a victim, when Pudgy was the one doing the setup. But Hansen recovered quickly, and played out the scene.

The others pushed back from the table, expecting a fight. Hansen pulled out his watch again. Ten P.M., on the mark.

He slowly gathered his winnings.

"Listen, it's only a game," he said. Pudgy puffed again, getting more and more red-faced. "I don't want any hard feelings," Hansen said. He motioned to a passing waiter. "Just calm down. Let me buy you a drink."

Pudgy took a deep breath, seemed to relax. The others sighed in relief.

Hansen took the bottle from the waiter's tray, led Pudgy to a vacant table in the back of the bar. Pudgy seemed stunned, and stumbled against Hansen. When they were seated, Hansen demanded, "What's the idea? Why not just give me the assignment directly, without all this nonsense?"

"The times are changing, Hansen." Pudgy was suddenly different. He no longer seemed nervous. His voice was strong, the hand holding the glass was steady. "Our boss is now working—officially at least—within the law. We have to be careful with our associations."

Hansen frowned.

"What do you know? You never rode with Culver. He would never be ashamed of any of us—"

Pudgy's hand moved with surprising speed, and held Hansen's arm in a viselike grip.

"All of our plans now call for circumspection. It is not a matter of shame, it is a matter of pragmatism." Hansen still looked confused, so Pudgy added, "Our boss has many enemies, so his plans and actions must be kept quiet. If you wish to continue to be valuable, you must play by his rules, even if you don't understand them. And one of the new rules is: Never use his name in connection with your business. Never."

Hansen shook off the offending hand. Pudgy seemed unconcerned.

"The money I let you win is yours. It is the advance for the job you are about to do."

Hansen hid his confusion behind another drink.

"We need you to find a man, and pick up a package. And to make sure the man who prepared the package . . . hmmm . . . finds his reward." He handed another envelope to Hansen under the table. "All the information you need is: in this envelope. Review it in private, then destroy it. You can relax tonight, choosing your own pleasures, but you will start on your assignment tomorrow morning."

He then stood, and said in a loud, slurred voice, "Thanks for the drink. No hard feelings!"

But Hansen had turned back to his drink, and nobody else seemed to notice the exchange. He finished his drink, then started back to Sally's.

Chapter 4

Hansen woke in the run-down cabin in Indian Territory. He was alone and had a terrible headache. He threw the empty bottle in his hand across the room, where it hit the wall with a hollow thud and bounced to the floor. It crashed into the other empty bottles and broke.

Hansen groaned. He wished he had a woman. His need was always strong, but his memories of the mountain women and the whores in New Hope had increased his desire. His job did have a time frame, but he could still work in a little detour. He was still his own man, after all. No harm could come from it. Culver would understand.

A patch of blue sky could be seen through the canvas covering the window. Hansen ripped off the torn material to get a better view. The storm had passed, but the sun had not yet risen. The hills to the east were just starting to lighten.

Hansen pivoted on the bed. His head felt as if it were splitting. He placed his foot firmly on the floor and considered his next move.

The cabin looked different in the early light than the night before. Now, Hansen could see the rust on the pipe of the old cookstove, the greasy black coating on the stove itself, the cobwebs in the corners of the dirt floor. The only neat thing in the cabin was O'Fallon's packs, stacked near the door.

Hansen rubbed his forehead and scowled. Where was the

stranger? Outside, as if from far away, Hansen heard a dull, rhythmic thud. He went to the door just as the sun crested the hills. The light almost blinded him, but he could make out O'Fallon on the hill. As Hansen's eyes adjusted to the light, he saw the body on the ground and O'Fallon's slow rhythm as he dug the grave.

The fool, Hansen thought. Doing all that work for nothing. The coyotes would have done the job for him.

Hansen scowled again. What should he do about the stranger? He was no threat. The gunfighter's memory of the night before was fuzzy, but Hansen could recall nothing being said that might be dangerous.

Hansen quickly saddled his horse and made one final look around the cabin. O'Fallon had taken his rifle with him, but his other gear was unguarded. Hansen grabbed the pack from which O'Fallon had pulled the booze the night before. He located another bottle and stuffed it into his own bags.

O'Fallon did not even look up from his work as Hansen rode away.

Hansen's destination was a small settlement about three days' ride into the Indian Territory. But he still had a few more days to reach there. He was in no particular hurry.

As the day wore on, the ground became less hilly and more grassy. The sun was low in the west when Hansen pulled on the reins, slowed the horse so that he could examine the landscape more closely.

The Indian Territory, while still sparsely populated, was not deserted, Hansen knew. The Indians of the Five Civilized Tribes—transplanted years before from the East—had formed some communities. The Cherokees had made their own nation. In addition, many pioneers of white or mixed blood dotted the landscape. Some had married into Indian families, or were in the area with the tacit approval of the Indians. Most were squatters, on the land illegally, indifferent to the wishes of the Indians. But where there were people in whatever numbers, there would be a woman.

Hansen stopped his horse, scanned the horizon. To his left, less than a mile away, he saw a stand of cottonwoods.

From experience, he knew this probably indicated a stream of some sort. If he followed the stream, he might come upon a house—and a woman.

He rode toward the green, watching the ground for other signs.

The tall grass had started to turn brown from the late summer sun. Wildflowers added blues and whites to the brown. The trees were starting to change colors. Hansen's mind, however, was not on the season.

He suddenly spotted what he had been searching for: a faint path through the grass, leading to the stream. It did not take a woodsman's eye to know the path was made by a man or a woman and not by rabbits or coyotes. He circled the area and found a deeper-worn path roughly following the water. Hansen turned his stallion along the path and watched the ground carefully.

This path had been well used, but he could not read sign well enough to know how many people walked this way. The path meandered through a meadow and some woods. The further Hansen traveled, the fainter the path became. So the gunfighter switched direction, with better luck.

In less than a half hour he could faintly smell wood smoke and cooking corn. This time, the path remained clear and the aroma of cooking became stronger the farther he rode.

Just around a curve of the path a small frame house came into view. It was located on a slight incline leading to a wide spot in the stream. The water was moving rapidly, reflecting sharp edges of light in the late afternoon. Hansen was coming in from the rear. Nobody was in sight, but a woman was singing on the other side of the building, near the water. Hansen dismounted, tied his horse to a tree. He pulled his revolver and cautiously looked around the house.

A young Indian woman was cooking corn on an open fire in a large black pot.

Hansen did not consider the woman pretty. She was wearing a plain dress and her hair was pulled back in a simple style. She was too skinny, with not enough curves. But she was a woman, and she seemed to be alone, which would make his pleasure that much easier.

Hansen's need was now so great that he could barely control himself.

The woman continued her soft singing. She apparently had not seen Hansen. He smiled. This was almost too easy!

He placed his revolver back in its holster. He quietly approached the woman.

Her back was toward him. The sun gleamed in her black, waist-length hair. As she stirred the pot with a smooth, rhythmic motion, her back swayed. Even though she was wearing a plain cotton dress, it sensually swished back and forth. The cloth shaped the woman's narrow waist and legs.

Hansen's heart beat faster as he neared the woman. Up close, she did not look so skinny, after all. He mentally removed her simple dress. He visualized the way her skin would look, naked against the sun, and how it would feel against him.

The woman tossed her head back and forth as a breeze blew off the water. Her long hair caressed her back.

Hansen imagined the touch of her hair against his skin.

Time seemed to be slowed for Hansen. He moved as if in a dream.

The woman turned. Her hair swept out in a long, graceful curve. It brushed against Hansen as her large, brown eyes looked up in surprise.

Hansen grabbed the woman by the shoulders and pulled her to him. Her breasts were pressed tightly against his chest. He could feel their firm outlines against him as he rubbed against her.

The woman's eyes widened. Her mouth opened to scream. Hansen clamped his mouth over hers. He ran his hands down her back, through her hair. She tried to bite, but Hansen was too strong. He pulled back his head, laughed, and stuck his hand in the back of the dress. With one strong motion he ripped off the buttons. He reached underneath the clothes and caressed the smooth skin.

The woman struggled. She pushed against Hansen, which

excited him even more. He liked his women to sometimes act as if they really didn't want him. He laughed again at this ridiculous thought. As he laughed, the woman started to scream again. Hansen again clamped his mouth over hers. He held her close against him, as she pounded his back with her small hands.

Hansen pulled her to the ground. But the woman was stronger than he had thought. She kicked, and managed to roll him over. She broke away for a few seconds. The gunfighter reached out, kicked her back to the ground. She landed on her knees. Hansen hit her on the side of the head. It snapped back, and she fell backward into the fire. The flames caught at her dress, but were extinguished as Hansen pulled her through the dust.

The woman tried to knee Hansen, but he caught her legs and spread them apart. He pushed up her dress to reveal the smooth skin, and loosened his pants. Hansen pushed himself against the woman. He had her pinned firmly to the ground, but she somehow moved sideways through the dirt.

Hansen threw the woman back to the ground, tried to hold her, though she was now fighting like a wild animal. He pushed the dress up further and pushed himself against the woman's slim body.

And then it was over, but only for a few minutes. Soon, Hansen would give the woman another chance.

"Don't worry about this one," he said, holding the woman solidly against the ground. "This was just a warm-up. We'll have plenty of time to get better acquainted."

He was already getting excited again. He loosened his grip for only a second, but it was long enough for the woman to free her hand. She reached out toward the pot and then made a quick, slashing motion. Hansen felt a cool streak along his face. He looked up and saw a butcher knife thrusting at him.

Hansen fell backward. The knife narrowly missed his throat.

His movement caused him to lose his grip. The woman was almost instantly on her feet. She had already smoothed her dress, and she held the knife at an upward angle, waiting for him.

Hansen felt wetness on his cheek. He touched it, and found blood on his hand.

Without any warning at all, the woman leaped forward and grabbed Hansen's crotch with a terrible grip and an even more terrible anger in her eyes.

Hansen, in shock, almost waited too long to react.

The knife slashed downward.

Hansen caught the woman's wrist with the knife in it, and twisted.

The woman kicked out, tripped the man, still holding on to him. Hansen grimaced in pain, but still gripped the hand with the knife. He twisted again, felt a crunch, and the woman loosened her hold on the knife and on him.

Hansen grabbed the weapon as it fell. Almost by instinct, he reversed the knife and pushed it hard into her small body.

It went deep through the cloth and skin.

Hansen pulled the blade from the woman and blood immediately soaked the front of the torn dress.

He pushed her away. She fell facedown by the stream. Her dark hair spilled into the water. The current pulled at it, making it seem alive.

Hansen stood for long seconds, breathing heavily, holding the knife. Blood ran into the stream, turning the water pink. The light breeze from the water was cool against his skin. He cursed. This had not been in his plans. None of the other women had ever put up that kind of fight. He hadn't even started to have any *real* fun with the Indian woman, and now she was dead.

Hansen pulled up his pants, thinking about his next step. Did the squaw have a man? Did she have any family? If so, they would be returning soon. They would also wind up dead if they tried to interfere, but he now preferred no more distractions.

He threw the knife into the stream and started to search the grounds.

The woman apparently had no livestock, except for a few

chickens, and he found no other tracks except for his and the woman's. Hansen next looked in the small house. It was clean and neat. The only furniture was two handmade chairs, a small table, a narrow pallet on the floor. A trunk and some shelves were along one wall.

Hansen guessed the woman lived alone, after all, so he had nothing more to worry about. By the time her body was found—if it was found—he would have completed his job and been long gone.

With his mind now at ease, he carelessly searched the trunk and the shelves, in case she had stashed money or other valuables. He found some quilts, a batch of newspaper clippings tied with string, a few small books, and other useless items. He tossed them to one side as he made his way through the home.

He found nothing he could use and no sign of any other person living in the small building.

Hansen stepped outside. Soon, it would be twilight. He could make another few miles before dark, and the delay would not cost him very much time. He walked back to his stallion, mounted, and continued his ride to the west.

He didn't bother to look back.

Chapter 5

The shovel made a rhythmic sound in the dawn light. Sean O'Fallon steadily dug the grave, not caring whether or not it disturbed Hansen's sleep. The wet dirt clung firmly to the metal, so from time to time O'Fallon had to strike the shovel blade against the ground to free the mud, making an even louder noise.

By O'Fallon's reckoning, he did not necessarily owe a decent burial to the dead man. After all, he had beaten a woman, tried to steal O'Fallon's goods, and then attempted to kill him. Still, Turk had been a man and deserved a better fate than to be left to the coyotes.

O'Fallon also reckoned that Jack Hansen would not deserve—and would not get—the same respect when his time came to die. And that time would be coming sooner than the gunfighter could know.

The decision was made the night before, almost on the spur of the moment, as Hansen blustered and bragged. O'Fallon had decided he would kill Jack Hansen. But it would be in O'Fallon's own time. He had waited years to finish paying off his debt to Culver's gang. He could afford to wait a little longer.

As he dug, O'Fallon's hatred became colder, harder, centered on the man in the cabin. The sun popped suddenly from behind the hills just as Hansen peered out the door of the cabin.

O'Fallon spotted the gunfighter, but the sight did not interrupt the grave digging.

Hansen obviously thought he was tough. And perhaps he was, if his opponents were women and unarmed men or if a gang was riding with him. Hansen obviously viewed O'Fallon with disdain, and believed that if he wanted he could kill the Tennessee man easily. But the night before he had been careless and had opened himself to attack any number of times. And how easy would it be now, with the sun blinding Hansen's eyes, for O'Fallon to simply pick up his rifle and pump three slugs into the supposedly tough man. That, however, would be too quick. Before Hansen died, O'Fallon wanted him to know who had killed him, and why he was dying. Besides, for a while at least, Hansen would be more valuable alive than dead.

He was the first solid lead to Culver that Sean had come across in years.

So O'Fallon continued to dig, even after Hansen went back inside the cabin.

The rifle was near. O'Fallon had quietly retrieved his Remington revolver from his bags during the night as Hansen slept in his drunken stupor. That gun was now in O'Fallon's waistband, under his shirt. He was familiar with men like Hansen and expected no trouble from him. Men like Hansen thought the whole universe was designed for their personal enjoyment. They were egotistical users, with no conscience or morals. They had no reservations about taking what they wanted, when they wanted. But they were also bullies. They preferred to shoot a man in the back rather than face him in a fair fight. Still, there was no use taking careless chances.

O'Fallon paused, leaning on the shovel to watch Hansen mount his horse and ride toward the west.

It would be an easy trail to follow.

The young man dug steadily until the hole was deep enough. He placed the body in the depression without comment and started to replace the dirt. He completed the work about midmorning, cleaned his shovel, and replaced it in his packs. He examined the bags, found his last bottle of whiskey missing. That had been expected. It was no great loss.

He dug deeper into the packs and pulled out an oilcloth that he had not opened the night before. He unwrapped the material to reveal a well-used holster. He strapped it on his right hip, then placed the Remington that had been in his waistband into the holster. O'Fallon did not like to advertise his skills, and a well-worn holster and revolver always seemed to invite a fight. He preferred to be let alone, to go his own way. Now, however, he knew he would soon be needing the gun.

The morning had turned out clear, bright, and dry. Consequently, his leg bothered him hardly at all, in spite of the previous day's events. The leg had stiffened up on him during the night, but the warmth of the cookstove had helped, as had the grave-digging exercise. Still, he practiced all his moves. He had to keep his skills sharp, and he had to stay limber.

He practiced his draw, over and over again, until the sound of metal against leather filled the air. He practiced from every angle: with the sun in his eyes and at his back; from a standing, a crouched, and a prone position; while running; single shots and several shots in succession. The Remington—originally a cap-and-ball model—had been converted for use with metal cartridges during the war. Ammunition was still expensive, but he ignored the cost and continued to practice, since in a fight an inch could mean the difference between life and death.

O'Fallon worked for most of the afternoon, developing his moves, and thinking about Hansen.

But most of all he was hating Culver.

Sean had been looking for Culver for years, ever since he had returned from the war and found his dreams shattered. But Culver was smart. He was elusive. He always seemed far from O'Fallon's grasp. It had gotten to the point where he was reduced to chasing rumors and hints of rumors, which is why he had traveled to Indian Territory.

The young man had no idea what to expect when Hansen

had joined him at the cabin the night before. Hansen's attitude and appearance made O'Fallon wary. The gunfighter did not scare O'Fallon, but he had just killed a man and was not anxious to kill two in one day. Hansen's presence in the territory seemed suspicious to O'Fallon, so he played along with Hansen's expectations and fed his ego to see what developed. Then he learned, almost by accident, of Hansen's association with Culver. O'Fallon almost grabbed the rifle and shot Hansen like a mad dog. But he soon realized that Hansen was a possible lead to Culver, and forced himself to remain calm and continue playing out the game. If he let Hansen live, his trail might lead back to Culver.

It was the only clue he had.

Also, after seeing Hansen's fear of fire—from lightning, from the lantern—O'Fallon decided that shooting Hansen would be too quick and painless. Hansen had ridden with Culver. Sean had no doubt that Hansen had been one of the men who had attacked and killed his wife and family during the war. Hansen and Culver deserved to die in as much pain as had their victims.

Hansen was not afraid of bullets, but he was afraid of fire.

What was Culver's worst fear? O'Fallon decided he would determine that, and prepare Culver's death accordingly.

Finally, satisfied with his practice session, O'Fallon cleaned his gun and inserted new cartridges. He packed and saddled his horses and started down the trail, following Hansen's sign. As expected, he had made no attempt to cover his trail and O'Fallon made good time.

At first, the trail made sense: a more or less straight line through Indian Territory. But then the trail started to zigzag in what at first seemed a random way. Had the gunfighter gotten lost? Was Hansen aware he was being trailed? Was he attempting to cut back for a possible ambush?

It took awhile for O'Fallon to realize that this was Hansen's amateurish way of looking for some sort of trail.

O'Fallon scanned the country around him but could see nothing out of the ordinary. He pushed on warily, but at a steady pace.

And then Hansen's tracks cut across another trail: a well-worn path following a stream. The water was running free and clear and the trees lining the banks had turned autumn colors. It was a nice stretch of ground, a good place for a homestead, O'Fallon thought.

As he continued to ride, however, O'Fallon grew more nervous. A good place for a homestead . . . a good place for a home . . . a good place to find a woman. His way with women had been one of the subjects Hansen bragged about most the night before. The realization hit O'Fallon hard: Hansen was looking for a woman just as he had when Culver's bunch found Sean's wife years before. O'Fallon kicked himself for not killing Hansen when he had the chance; he never should have let the gunfighter live.

The trail no doubt led to a homestead. O'Fallon urged his animals to greater speed. Then he thought he saw a trace of pink in the water. It could have been from the setting sun, but the young man spurred his horse, disregarding the loaded pack animal following behind. He had the terrible feeling he was too late, again.

O'Fallon's fears were confirmed as he rounded the curve of the path. The fire under the pot had almost burned out. The blood on the ground was still damp, but drying fast.

The woman, almost facedown in the creek, was motionless.

O'Fallon jumped off his horse, ran to the still figure, gently rolled her over. She was unconscious, but alive. The wound looked deep. She had lost a lot of blood. Her skin was cold to the touch.

Hansen had apparently worked fast. He had ridden into the homestead, probably raped the woman, and fled, all within a few hours. O'Fallon cursed himself for his leisurely pace. If he had ridden faster he might have been able to stop Hansen.

The woman, however, had apparently put up a struggle. The ground was torn and several patches of blood dotted the ground.

The stream bank was muddy. O'Fallon needed someplace

dry to put the woman. He ran inside the small house, decided the table would do the job. He cleared off the plate and cup, the salt container, the dishpan. He stripped the sheets from the bed, spread them on the table, and tore some of them into bandages.

Back outside, he kicked the fire to stir up the embers, threw on some more sticks, and placed a kettle to boil.

All this took only a few moments.

He gently lifted the woman from the mud and moved her to the table. It had been a cool day, so fortunately few flies were buzzing. Had it been even a few weeks earlier, during the heat of the summer, the wound could have easily become infected. As it was, she still had a chance.

O'Fallon arranged the woman on the table, and realized the woman was lucky in still another way.

Hansen had spared her face.

The woman was very pretty, but O'Fallon's examination was clinical as he loosened the dress. He looked carefully at the wound. Some blood was still seeping out, but it was relatively clean. The knife had gone in straight, without twisting, which had limited internal damage.

O'Fallon brought in the boiling kettle, washed the bandages, cleaned the wound. Bleeding started again, so he applied direct pressure with a clean bandage. The blood seeped through, but O'Fallon did not release the pressure until the bleeding had stopped.

It was dark when O'Fallon was through.

He lit a short candle and searched for fresh bedding. He found some clean sheets and blankets that had been stored in a chest that Hansen had obviously ransacked. O'Fallon moved the woman to the freshly made bed and covered her with a blanket. He brought the candle close to her face. She was breathing slowly, but steadily. For the moment, he had done all he could.

He stepped outside into the cool night air and stretched. He felt very tired. He walked to the stream, splashed cold water on his face, then cleaned the blood off his hands and arms. The sounds of crickets and frogs filled the area and

A COLD, DARK TRAIL

O'Fallon thought again, This would be a good place for a homestead.

He took a deep breath and returned to the house.

The woman was sleeping. She had a pretty face: high cheekbones, framed by black hair against the white pillow.

The damp air started to cool the inside of the building, so O'Fallon started a fire in the old stove to avoid the possibility of shock. He kept the fire small, but steady, from the bundle of dry wood stacked next to the stove.

After making sure the woman was warm and resting as well as could be expected, O'Fallon turned his attention to the cabin. The small candle cast little light, but it was enough to pick out the room's details. He found canned goods, and empty jars that were apparently intended to hold some of the food being cooked in the outside pot. He found cooking utensils, women's clothes, books. In one book was a marriage certificate—Jim and Maria Rushing—and what seemed to be an old land deed.

In the bottom of the trunk he found men's clothes that apparently had not been worn for several years. An old black powder rifle stood in the corner.

O'Fallon put things back as best he could. When he turned, he kicked a stack of newspaper clippings. He picked them up and examined them by candlelight. Most were in a strange script; Sean guessed they were Cherokee publications. A few were in English, and discussed the politics of the Cherokee tribe during the war, and especially the man named Jim Rushing—the woman's husband. One of the clippings described how he had been killed by an assassin's bullet during the war.

O'Fallon tied the papers back together and placed them on the chest.

The woman suddenly groaned and seemed to awaken for a moment. Sean rushed to her side, but she had turned her head slightly and already fallen back to sleep.

O'Fallon rearranged the covers up past her bare shoulders to her neck. Her pulse was steady, and her skin was no longer cold to the touch.

The young man pulled a chair next to the bed and took one of her hands in his. Her hand seemed stiff, small, and cold.

He sat quietly through the night, holding her hand, and occasionally throwing another stick on the fire.

Chapter 6

Jack Hansen met no further delays after his brief encounter with the Indian woman. He made good time, even though his pace was slowed some by his decision to cover his trail for the first few miles—just in case he was mistaken and the squaw did have a man. He was not particularly worried, but he preferred to take no more chances. This was a relatively simple job, and he wanted to get it over with as quickly as possible so that he could return to civilization and more pleasurable pursuits.

Hansen's destination was a small settlement in the Cherokee Nation called Parkersburg in the heart of Indian Territory. His assignment was to pick up a package that consisted of collected land-survey notes and records made by an engineer named Josiah Quincy, and eliminate the owner of the package. The assignment had to be completed by September 28. Hansen was to send a telegram indicating his success, and then return to St. Louis with the information no later than October 5.

Even with the delay due to the Indian woman, Hansen would have plenty of time to track down Quincy, get the goods, catch a train, and arrive in St. Louis with at least a week to spare. He was already thinking about the soft bed and warm women waiting for him.

He hit Parkersburg about three days after he left the woman in the creek. It was a cool midafternoon. His stallion pranced proudly down the dusty street—really, little more than a wide path—into the settlement. Hansen knew that Parkersburg was a Cherokee town, but that fact meant little to him. He was amazed at how much Parkersburg resembled a white man's town: houses, stores, churches, even a school. He found no obvious hint that this was Indian country.

The only real difference between this town and those east of the Indian Territory border was the new appearance of most of the buildings. Parkersburg, like many of the towns in the territory (and in the states, for that matter), had been virtually destroyed during the war. It was now being rebuilt from the ground up. It was a slow process, however, because the Cherokee Nation had allied itself with the losing side in the war. Rebuilding funds were scarce and most of the buildings were of rough, unpainted wood. The only exception was the brick school in the center of town.

Some of the children pointed as he rode past. They watched him for a few minutes, then went back to their play. One of them tried to follow. Hansen thought, Come on out, brat. I'd love to teach you a lesson. But then the boy turned and again joined his playmates.

Hansen stopped his horse in front of a wooden structure a few blocks from the school. It was a little larger than most of the other buildings in town, but was made of the same rough material. A sign over the store said, Parker's Store. Two Indians, both dressed like white men, were lounging on the wooden front porch. No horses were in front of the building, but Hansen could see several in a small corral at a livery down the street.

Hansen dismounted, wrapped the reins around a post on one side of the porch.

The younger of the two Indians said, in English, "Think he's another damned surveyor? Seems like they're—"

The second Indian placed his hand on the other's elbow, motioning for silence. The first man, aware he was speaking too loudly, lowered his voice. He mumbled something, and the older man answered in their native language. Both Indians shrugged, closed their eyes, and leaned back against the wall. From down the street, dozens of children suddenly came yelling and running in all directions. Hansen's boots made a hollow sound as he stepped onto the porch and into the building. The Indians did not look at him again.

The interior of the store was dark, shadowed, and smelled of old leather. Barrels of flour and coffee were arranged to the right of the door. Colin Parker, the owner of the business, stood behind the counter. Canned goods were stacked along the back wall, almost hidden by his bulk. An old, greasy-looking white man was slouched at a table in the left corner of the room. A big yellow dog was stretched on the floor. Hansen kicked the dog out of the way. The animal jumped, circled the room, and cautiously lay down in a curtained back doorway.

"Stranger, my name's Parker. What might I do for you?"

His voice boomed out, filling the room. It was not an entirely friendly voice. Parker was a big man, with medium-long black hair and a nose that had apparently been the victim of a number of fights.

"I'll start with a shot of your best," Hansen said.

Parker's bare arms did not move from their resting place on the counter. He said, "I don't normally serve liquor. Especially to strangers."

"I don't give a damn. Just pour me a shot. How about sometime today?" Hansen said.

Hansen's sarcasm was lost on the storekeeper. He finally lumbered over to another section of the counter, pulled out a bottle. Hansen guessed that Parker was the kind of man that kept a sawed-off shotgun next to the rotgut.

"When I do sell, it's only by the bottle," Parker said. Hansen reached for the bottle, but it wouldn't budge: Parker's large hand remained wrapped solidly around it. "We don't get many strangers around here, so it's nothing personal, but the rule is no credit."

Hansen smiled, but he was starting to feel irritated. He said nothing, but pulled out a silver dollar, laid it on the counter. Only then did Parker release his grip on the bottle and sweep up the coin in one fluid motion.

Hansen poured a drink, swallowed, and poured another. He needed information, so held up the bottle and said, "Join me for a drink?"

Parker's fists remained solidly on the bar.

"I never touch the stuff."

Hansen shrugged. Maybe he shouldn't have kicked the dog. He poured another drink and said, "I'm just being friendly."

Outside, a young boy jumped onto the porch, calling out in an Indian tongue. One of the Indians sitting on the porch answered. The older Indian stayed put, but the younger man followed the child down the street. Parker seemed to be listening to the exchange.

"Not bad whiskey," Hansen said.

Parker responded, "I didn't catch your name."

"Jack Hansen." The name was relatively well known, but Parker's face showed no recognition. The smile was set in his face.

"Well, Hansen, I assume you are just passing through. If you need supplies, I'll be happy to do business with you, and see you on your way."

Hansen didn't like being pushed. He looked around, decided this town was just like any other, and not worth his contempt. He had plenty of time to complete his job, and there were a lot of other places where information was exchanged. Maybe he could kill two birds with one stone.

"Which way to your whorehouse, Parker?"

His smile was wolfish, just daring Parker to come back at him. But Parker said nothing. He only lost his smile.

"I've been on the trail a long time," Hansen continued. "You know how it is."

Parker pushed away from the counter and said, "I run a clean business, and this is a clean town. The Cherokee Nation does not need your 'civilized' ways." He paused, then added, "Finish your drink. I expect you to be gone by the time I get back."

The store owner turned, walked through the door to the porch. The dog followed, growling softly as he passed.

Hansen laughed.

Outside, Parker sat on the edge of the porch where he could talk with the older Indian but could also watch Hansen. The two men on the porch were mumbling to each other. Hansen could not make out the words. He laughed again and poured another drink.

"You can buy me a drink, Mr. Hansen."

It was the old man at the table.

"Old Parker is kind of peculiar. He's full-blooded Cherokee, you know, but educated from back East. Makes for a strange combination sometimes."

"Yeah. Sure."

"Now, old Beech, he's not like that. No, sir! I'd be happy to have a drink with you."

"Especially if I buy the whiskey."

"Well, I tell you true, Mr. Hansen, old Beech has been down on his luck and has to rely on the charity of others. I have seen better days."

The old drunk was in his seventies, or older. He was wearing a buckskin suit worn thin by years of use. His gray, bristly beard covered pale, shrunken cheeks. His voice was hoarse. Hansen did not like to be with sick, old men and had started to turn away when Beech added, "Besides, I have some information you might be able to use."

"Okay, Beech, you bought yourself a drink." Hansen filled the glass. "Let's hear what you have to say."

Beech drank greedily, choked, coughed.

"Old Parker's a strange one," Beech wheezed. "But he's been through a lot, as maybe we all have. He has his own ways. Just as we all have."

Beech looked at Hansen with runny eyes.

"Even you, Mr. Hansen, have your ways that others may not understand. But does that make them better than anybody else's? Or worse?"

"You've had your drink. I'm still waiting for the information."

"What I'm trying to say, Mr. Hansen, is that you may have stronger needs, shall we say, than some others. Like old Beech. He once needed a lot of women. But those days are passed." He cackled. "But those were the days!"

"Go on."

"Now, old Parker, his needs may be just as great, but he's married to a woman who knows how to treat a man. So he doesn't necessarily understand what it's like for the rest of us. But old Beech, he's spent a lot of time alone, and he understands. Yes, sir, old Beech understands whoring. Parker would never tell you what you need to know, because he doesn't understand. You ask me, and I can tell you!"

Hansen waited for Beech to continue, moving his glass in circles on the rough table. He felt impatient, but he knew that sometimes babbling old fools could provide unexpected information. He said, "Talk plain. Do you know where I can find a woman, or don't you?"

Beech tentatively reached for the bottle. Hansen didn't stop him. "Old Beech is too old for that kind of fun, but I hear a lot and see a lot," the old man said. "So I can tell you where to get what you need. Last woman tried to set up shop, Parker ran her right out of town. With a horsewhip! Damnedest thing I've ever seen: her gown flapping in the breeze, exposing her behind for all the world to see—for free!—and old Parker snapping that whip. The tip never touched her, you see, but it scared the holy bejeebers out of her!"

He cackled again. Parker and the Indian glanced inside, then went back to their own talk. Hansen said, "Doesn't do me much good now, does it?"

"Well, sir, let old Beech finish the story! That woman has no more left the territory than I have! She just set up shop about twenty miles from here. She can sure take care of you, Mr. Hansen! Wish I was twenty years younger. I'd like to give that filly a ride, for sure!"

"Yeah, that's worth the drink." Hansen continued to move his glass in circles. "How would you like to earn another bottle?" Beech's runny eyes looked up eagerly at Hansen. "I'm looking for some other information, as well. I'm supposed to meet an old friend. His name's Quincy. Supposed to be working around here."

Beech cackled.

"Hell, yes, everybody knows Quincy. He's been in everybody's talk for months, but he doesn't talk, no sir! He probably works for the railroad. I imagine they'll come through, no matter what Parker and his bunch want!" He lowered his voice. "Does he work for the railroad?"

"Can't tell you. Do you want the bottle or not?"

"Quincy comes in, and he goes. He buys his supplies with gold. He stays out in the wilds for weeks at a time. Who knows what he's up to? He's been here since April, and hangs his hat at a little shack, about seven miles northwest of here. Only problem is, the whore is southeast of here. Maybe you could look up both?"

Hansen had heard enough. He smiled and pushed away from the table, leaving the bottle for Beech. Outside, the porch roof cast long shadows on the wood planks of the floor. Hansen tossed another silver dollar to Parker.

"Another bottle for old man Beech." Parker raised his eyebrows. "Guess I'm getting soft in the head. But I did have an enjoyable conversation with the old fool."

"And you, Hansen?"

"I'm just passing through, remember? I need nothing more from anybody here. I'll probably be heading for the southeast."

"So Beech spilled his guts to you about the whore."

Hansen laughed.

"He and I understand each other!" he said.

The older Indian looked at Hansen blankly. Parker spit off the porch, raising a small cloud of dust. Hansen, however, had already started his ride to the northwest to finish his business in Indian Territory.

Chapter 7

Sean O'Fallon woke about midnight. The fire had burned low, giving a slight chill to the air.

He stood, stretched, and then checked the bandages. The bleeding had stopped hours before, and the wound already seemed slightly better. Earlier in the night, the woman had experienced a slight fever, which seemed to have broken. O'Fallon was glad; he had been afraid she would be dead by morning, but now it seemed she might live. He adjusted the covers. The woman turned, and moaned, but her hands and face remained warm.

Sean crossed the room, tossed some more sticks into the stove. The fire popped, hissed, sparked, sent the smell of wood smoke into the air. The metal creaked softly as it heated. O'Fallon warmed his leg, which was still slightly sore, before returning to his chair to continue his wait.

The woman suddenly opened her eyes. They were a dark brown, deep and lovely in the gentle glow of the stove, watching without fear or surprise. By simply watching, they hinted at great depths.

O'Fallon said softly, "How do you feel?"

She blinked, turned her head slightly.

"Who are you?"

The words were few, but revealed a clear, songlike quality.

"My name is Sean O'Fallon. I found you in the stream. I am a friend."

She moaned softly and said, "It hurts. But I'll live. You did a good job. Thank you." She leaned her head back on the pillow and was almost immediately asleep again.

The next time she woke was early the following morning. O'Fallon had gone outside and collected a handful of eggs. When he returned, the woman was sitting up with the blankets wrapped around her. He was so surprised that he almost dropped the eggs.

"What are you doing?" he demanded. "You're hurt badly. You lost a lot of blood. You shouldn't be sitting up like that."

She grimaced.

"I'm of hearty stock. I wasn't raised to sit in bed all day and be waited on like an invalid."

O'Fallon gently, but firmly, guided her back down on the bed.

"Your mother no doubt raised you right, but if you're not careful you'll open that wound again."

"Mr. O'Fallon, thank you for your help, but—"

"Sean. My name is Sean. Tell me your name."

"Maria Rushing."

"Let me take another look at that wound. It's probably time for a new bandage." Maria hesitated for an instant, so O'Fallon added, "I don't mean to be pushy, but I think you had better trust me. If I wanted to take advantage of you, I would have done so last night."

Maria relaxed, and even had a hint of a smile on her face, which surprised Sean for the second time in the space of only a few minutes. How could a woman smile after being so brutally attacked and left for dead?

"Of course. I'm sorry."

Sean gently turned down the covers, loosened the bloodsoaked bandages. They tried to stick to her skin, so O'Fallon heated some more water and moistened them. Still, Maria winced as he removed the cloth. The wound seemed to be drawing together, but was still an ugly red. He washed the dried blood from around the wound.

"It's raw," he said as he worked. "But it could be a lot worse. I've seen a lot worse."

"In the war?"

"In the war." O'Fallon rinsed the bloody bandages and dried the tender skin. "Do you know who did this to you?"

"I don't know his name. He sneaked up and attacked me from behind. But I got a good look at him. He was about as tall as you, but was wearing dusty black clothes and had a mustache. He tried to rape me, but I had a knife and almost deprived him of his manhood."

"I bet that took him by surprise. He's not used to attacking women without the help of a gang behind him. His name's Jack Hansen. I've been trailing him for about twenty miles. It's a long story. Right now, it's time to rebandage that wound. . . ."

"Wait."

O'Fallon paused, bandages in hand.

"Outside, in the shed, are some herbs hanging from the ceiling. Boil some fresh water and bring me the plants."

"But your shoulder . . ."

"I trusted you. Now you trust me."

O'Fallon washed and filled the pan from the stream, placed it on the stove, then went for the plants. They were brown, shriveled, unrecognizable. When he brought them inside, Maria explained, "The old ways are not entirely forgotten. My people know of medicines and cures that were old before your people ever suspected this land existed. Hand me the plants and that bowl over there on the cupboard. We're going to make a poultice for this wound." And then, in response to O'Fallon's dubious look, she said, "The effort won't hurt my shoulder, and only I know the proper combination. Trust me."

Maria crumpled the plants into a fine dust, then instructed O'Fallon to add the boiling water. She watched him walk from the bed to the stove and then mix the poultice.

"Sean, you were in the war?"

"Yes."

"And you were wounded in the war."

"Yes."

"You walk with a limp. Perhaps I could help you heal, as well?"

"The doctors said I would never walk again. I've done pretty well on my own. I don't think I need any help."

O'Fallon mixed the ingredients, following Maria's instructions. Under her guidance, O'Fallon applied the herbal paste and fresh bandages. She grimaced again, but did not cry out. When O'Fallon was through, he pulled the covers back over the woman. She closed her eyes and her breathing slowed.

"Sean O'Fallon?"

Her voice was soft.

"Yes?"

"This man, Hansen, who did this to me. You are following him for a reason. He did something far worse to you than he did to me?"

"Yes. How do you know?"

"I saw it in your eyes. I then question your judgment, wasting valuable time here, taking care of me, when you could be going after him."

"The time's not wasted. He leaves an easy trail to follow. I'll get him."

A moment of silence passed. Then, as Maria opened her eyes, O'Fallon saw in them a rare determination.

"Very well, then. Tomorrow we will go."

"I can't leave you alone. You're still too weak."

"We will go."

O'Fallon made the woman rest as he prepared a gruel of broth and corn meal to feed her. She slept the rest of the day, and woke in the evening only long enough to take some more food and to change the bandage. O'Fallon was surprised at how quickly she seemed to gain back her strength and how the wound was pulling together. She slept peacefully through the night, so Sean spread his blanket on the porch.

The following morning, O'Fallon received still another surprise. While it was still dark, he woke to the aroma of biscuits baking from inside the house. He jumped from his pallet and said, "What the hell are you doing?" He rushed inside, then regretted his harsh words. Maria was moving steadily, if slowly, and O'Fallon had to admire her courage. His voice became more gentle.

"Just what do you think you're doing? Trying to kill yourself?"

"I'm preparing for our trip."

"You're in no condition to travel."

Maria smiled, as if she were in on some joke, and said, "What if I told you the wound is nearly healed?"

"I'd say you were crazy."

"Come here, and look for yourself."

She sat on the edge of the bed and opened her shirt without embarrassment. O'Fallon again loosened the bandages, and was shocked to see the wound healing quickly and cleanly.

"Well, Sean, are you satisfied? The medicinal herbs help the body to heal itself. Now I need exercise. Let me finish the packing. You can go prepare the livestock. My horse is in a meadow, up the creek."

"I'll admit you're healing fast. But you can't go with me."

"I know. You have traveled alone for so long, you are not sure you can work with another. I respect that. But because of me you lost valuable time. I know this area intimately, and can help you find your way quicker. I can help you find shortcuts. And I know the people, which could give you an edge over Hansen." She smiled again. "Besides, I will come anyway: I don't believe you would attempt to force me away with violence."

Maria's small horse was grazing, unpenned and unshod. He curried the animals, fed them a little from his supplies. The rest had done his horses good. They had been on the trail for many months, and had been tired. Now, they seemed anxious to move on.

O'Fallon brought a bucket of fresh water from the stream. The stars were still visible overhead, and a slight trace of red appeared in the east. Inside, Maria was removing biscuits from the pans, humming softly to herself. For a moment O'Fallon felt a warmth he had not felt in years. He quickly stifled the feeling. Stiffly, he placed the bucket down, grabbed the canteens, and retreated back to the stream.

For the first time in years, he again felt like crying, but he did not. He pushed his feelings firmly back in place. By the time he got back to the house, his canteens full, he was again in control.

Maria had set the table.

"Have breakfast before we leave."

Rather than argue, O'Fallon sat down with Maria. The biscuits were light and brown. The gravy was smooth. It was better than any of his own trail cooking.

Maria looked around the cabin and said, "Before the war, Jim and I owned hundreds of acres. It was a fine farm, and we also had a home in the capital, for the times when Jim was on official business. Now, I have only a few acres, which I am about to leave behind." She looked straight at O'Fallon. "A person cannot cling to the past forever. We must make peace and move on. I am ready."

The two made good time, even traveling slowly enough to keep from aggravating Maria's wound. Hansen's trail was easy to follow, in spite of zigzags and clumsy attempts to cover his tracks. And when it became apparent that Hansen was headed toward Parkersburg, Maria did in fact know of several shortcuts.

As O'Fallon and Maria rode, side by side, they quickly fell into a routine that was almost pleasant: riding, exchanging conversation, breaking for meals, resting, and camping in the evening. O'Fallon found himself talking comfortably of his background, and he learned of Maria's life. Her husband had been a leader in the nation; at one time he was even an adviser to Chief John Ross. He advocated neutrality during the war. The forces opposing him, however, were too powerful. Jim Rushing was assassinated and the nation allied itself with the Confederates.

"We all lost, but the nation lost most of all," Maria said. "Before the war, Jim and I were fairly well off, but after he got killed I lost interest. I had to get away, by myself, for a while. I think now that maybe it is time to stop running."

On the third night of the trip, the two were talking after they had completed supper and cleaned the dishes. The moon was shining, and both were relaxed. The evening had turned cool. Maria was healing extraordinarily quickly, but still had an occasional chill. This night, she was huddled near the fire, shivering, in spite of herself. O'Fallon poured them both another cup of coffee and then sat down beside her on the blanket. He put his arm around her. It was the first time he had touched Maria since the first night, when he had held her hand as she slept. She did not push him away.

"I can't help but shiver a little," she said.

"It's all right. Considering what you've been through, you're lucky to be alive, much less well enough to be on the trail. A little shiver seems allowed."

Then, to O'Fallon's surprise, Maria spread her blanket around them and rested her head on his shoulder. He stiffly caressed her silky black hair.

"You make me feel good, Sean O'Fallon. And I have met few men who could do that."

The woman seemed to relax, then, and continued her talk. "Jim could make me feel good; he could make me laugh, and he could make me feel secure."

"You must have loved him very much."

"He was a good man, but he was caught in the middle. Jim had high ideals—strange, I think, for a politician. He tried to act on what he believed to be right. But there were too many factions, too many enemies, and Jim was killed. Yet, I have to admire him for doing what he believed to be right." She paused, then added, "You are a lot like Jim in many ways. Yet, you're different. I have never met a person quite like you."

"It seems such a lonely life. Such a beautiful woman as you, yet never to have a family, to always be alone. . . ."

O'Fallon's voice trailed off. Maria answered, quietly, "You're speaking more of yourself than of me."

"No."

"You have been hurt very badly. You cannot hide it from

me. I see the hurt on your face." She paused, then said, "It is not really Hansen that you are after, is it?"

"No. Hansen was a member of the gang that . . . attacked and killed my wife during the war. I swore vengeance on the leader of the gang."

"And you are still looking for this man? How cold is this dark trail? How long ago did you lose your wife? And how long can you carry the grief with you?"

Maria felt very warm next to him, and suddenly Sean felt scared. The woman's face, lit by orange light from the campfire, was turned up to him. Her brown eyes were searching his. Her skin was smooth to his touch. Her breath was warm, sweet, inviting. Almost in spite of himself, O'Fallon leaned forward. His lips met hers, and she did not pull back. She put her arm around his neck and pulled him closer. He kissed her gently, and she returned the kiss. He felt warm inside, as familiar feelings returned. . . .

Without warning, O'Fallon gently pushed the woman back. He said, "No. Not yet." He stood, awkwardly. Maria watched O'Fallon, but his shadow hid her face. He said, "I'm . . . sorry."

"Yes. I understand."

O'Fallon remained motionless, standing stiffly. Maria reached up, took his hand in hers.

"Just remember you do not have to remain alone. There is a time for pain, a time for grief. And there is a time to let go of the pain."

Maria pulled the blanket around her and stretched out on the ground. O'Fallon threw another stick on the fire and stretched out on his own blanket, on the other side of the fire. He watched Maria's still, dark figure through the bright orange flames and remembered better times. . . .

It was a warm day in September 1863. Sean was sitting on a pile of leaves that had been dried by the bright sun shining through the partially naked branches. Rain had forced many of the leaves from the trees a few days before. The eighteen-year-old impatiently watched the slow-moving creek running past the old oak.

Sean wore a homespun shirt and pants. His wool jacket now rested beside him on the ground. His body was muscular, developed through honest, hard work. The muscles in his arms were well defined as he easily pushed himself up off the ground. He looked nervously around him again.

He smiled broadly when he spotted Laura running to him. Her long blonde hair curled upon her shoulders. Her green eyes twinkled. She was wearing the silver locket he had brought home from town to celebrate their "anniversary."

Sean laughed, hugged her close. He said, "You look like an angel!"

"You asked me all the way out here to tell me that?" Laura said. Her tone was playful. Her breasts pushed warmly against Sean's chest. The clean scent of her hair, the touch of her skin, excited him. He kissed her. She returned the kiss, then, laughing, pushed him back and said, "That is the Sean O'Fallon I love!" But then she looked into his eyes and saw a sadness she had never seen before.

"What's wrong?"

"I've made a decision. I'm leaving in a week to fight for the Union."

She pulled away.

"I knew you would. But why? They don't need you. They'll win the war without you."

"I've thought about it for a long time." He caressed Laura's hair. "My older brothers went, and sacrificed their lives. Victory still is not guaranteed, and every man must play his part. And I owe it to you. I want our home to be safe. I want our children to be safe, and free. My grandparents came here to be free, and fought during the Revolution for freedom. If even one man is a slave, how can any of us be free?"

Laura said nothing.

"And you know I've never run from a fight in my life," Sean continued. "If I wasn't a fighter, I never would have won you."

Laura tried to return to the teasing way she'd had earlier.

"You haven't won me yet! My father still hasn't given permission for us to marry. And now, with you going to war . . ."

"Are you against me on this?"

She fell back into Sean's arms.

"All I ever wanted was to be your wife," she said. "You know I will wait until your return."

"So you still want to marry me?"

"Of course. But the circuit rider won't be here again for a month, even if Daddy would give his permission. . . ."

"I'm of age. You're of age. Will you marry me? Would you marry me today? Tell me yes or no."

Her voice was a whisper. "Yes."

Sean whooped, picked up Laura in his arms, and ran over the hill to where his saddled horse was tied.

"What's this?"

"We're getting married! A preacher is passing through Jenkins City, only a half-day's ride from here. We'll be there by afternoon!"

She pounded him on the chest, and said, "Put me down, Sean O'Fallon! Put me down!"

He stopped dead in his tracks. He set her gently on the ground, looking dejected. He said, "What's wrong? I thought you wanted to marry me."

Then she whooped, laughed mischievously, and raced for the horse.

"Well, what are we waiting for? We've got a whole week before you're leaving. Let's not waste a minute!"

Sean ran over, pulled her to him, and kissed her again. Her mouth was warm against his. Her body was soft and loving against his.

He jumped on the horse, grabbed Laura's arm, and helped her up. Her hair tickled him as he kissed her neck and said, "Just you see, this will be the start of a wonderful life!"

And they both laughed in the sunshine.

Chapter 8

Sean O'Fallon heard a slight moan. He rolled out from under his blanket, pulled his revolver, and called out, "Laura!" But when he opened his eyes he saw Maria, huddled in the blankets across from the embers of the fire.

His heart was beating fast. He holstered his gun and forced himself to calm down. He had been dreaming, again. He could control his emotions, but he could not control his dreams, which sometimes seemed more real than his day-to-day life. He rose, threw some more sticks on the fire, and placed his blanket over Maria.

He slept fitfully the rest of the night.

Maria became stronger as they rode, and the two made even faster time. When they hit Parkersburg, Hansen's trail was still fresh; they weren't over two hours behind him.

"He's here," O'Fallon said. "I can feel it."

"You'll soon find him. And then?"

O'Fallon shrugged. He had been following Culver's trail for so long that O'Fallon no longer thought past the time when he would catch up to Culver. Some of Culver's gang had been local men. O'Fallon had hunted down the ones he knew about, and pieced together information about the identities of some of the others who had participated in the rape and murder of his wife. Many still remained unidentified. O'Fallon had known all along that chances were slim for catching up with all of Culver's gang, which was why his pain and hatred had been directed to the leader of the group. Based on Hansen's own words, he no doubt had been one of those who murdered O'Fallon's wife, and he was determined to kill Hansen in the most terrible way possible, even though the Tennessee man still held Culver ultimately responsible.

Yet, something in Sean caused him doubts. Would he be able to kill Hansen in cold blood? The hatred still burned in O'Fallon, and Hansen's attack on Maria should make the job easier. But a lot of years had passed since O'Fallon had returned home. Revenge at first had been neither easy nor hard; he had moved as if in a dream, as the pain blocked out all other feelings. Now the hurt was of a different sort. Had Maria picked up on this hesitation? What did she really think of his search? Did she find it a weakness? O'Fallon almost wished that this encounter, which he had been working toward for so long, was already over.

"This doesn't look like the pictures they paint of Indian villages back East," Sean said.

Maria smiled. "The Cherokee have adopted many of the white men's ways. We farm, live in towns, are businessmen, lawyers, and politicians." As the two rode down the dusty street, they approached a large brick building. "At the same time, we take pride in our culture," Maria said. "We've tried to provide for our children, in spite of the ravages of war. Colin Parker, the son of the founder of this town, received his basic education in Cherokee schools, as did I, and then attended an Eastern college until the war started. The war was hard on the family, and Colin runs the family store, but he is also trying to revive the town. He caused that school to be rebuilt almost before work on any the homes or businesses started."

Since O'Fallon had left the Tennessee mountains, he had seen and learned more than he could have dreamed about in his youth. Yet, he felt as if he had barely scratched the surface. O'Fallon had never before known a woman like Maria. She was so young, yet so self-confident; possessing a better education than even the few teachers in Tennessee; already a widow, but without bitterness. And Sean wondered about her people: independent, proud, refusing to give up. O'Fallon suspected their days as an independent nation were numbered, but still they planned and built for the future.

Maria glanced up at him and smiled. O'Fallon turned away, confused.

Some children were playing in the schoolyard. One pointed at Maria and O'Fallon, whispered something to another of the children, then took off down the street in a trail of dust. Maria smiled at the sight. O'Fallon tried not to notice the children. They reminded him of the family he would never have.

Further down the street was a general store.

"That is Colin Parker's place," Maria said. "He'll know who's been in town and when. He doesn't miss much."

Parker and the child, along with a couple of other Indians, were waiting on the porch of the building. Maria smiled.

"Colin! I see you still have nothing better to do than laze around on the front porch!"

"Maria! It's good to see you again. For you, I'll take a few minutes from my busy schedule!"

The woman gracefully swung off her small horse. The boy caught the reins as they fell. Parker swept Maria up in his big arms.

"Your boy is getting big," she said, and took his hand in hers. "Last I saw him, he was barely a toddler."

"I've had two more since you left," Parker said.

"Another few years and you can populate this town just with your family!"

O'Fallon felt uncomfortable, and jealous in spite of himself. He was envious of Maria's friends and of Parker's family, but his face revealed no emotion as the two old friends chatted.

"When little Matt," Parker pointed to the boy, "came running, said another stranger was in town—this one with a woman—I wondered if it might be you. For some reason, I've been thinking about you this afternoon." His voice boomed. Then he suddenly realized the lumps under Maria's dress were bandages and his voice grew quiet. He looked at

Maria, at O'Fallon, at the revolver O'Fallon wore at his side, and back at Maria.

"What happened?" Parker finally said.

"A thug named Hansen." She took O'Fallon by the arm and continued, "My friend, Sean O'Fallon, was trailing Hansen to partially settle an old debt when he found me, almost dead, after Hansen attacked me."

Parker looked her over.

"Almost dead? O'Fallon's a good doctor, then."

"He's a good man."

"I should have shot the bastard when I had the chance," Parker said to O'Fallon. "You just missed Hansen. The son of a bitch came in for a drink, and I thought he was going to start some kind of trouble. Then he calmed down, and got talkative, but I wasn't in the mood. The only one who would listen to him was—" He whirled and yelled through the open door, "Beech! Get out here!"

Some grumbling and cursing came from inside the building, followed by the scraping of a chair against the floor. An old man with runny eyes stumbled to the door.

"Whatcha yelling at ole Beech for?" He swayed, squinted at the sunlight, obviously drunk.

"You had a long talk with Hansen. What's he up to?"

Beech cackled.

"Hell if I know . . . I just wanted a drink out of him. I wasn't listening very closely."

O'Fallon urged, "What was he looking for? What kind of questions did he ask?"

Beech cackled again, then lowered his head to look at the dusty street.

"Answer the question, if you want any more credit in this town," Parker said.

"Oh, what the hell. He asked about Madame Janey's whorehouse. And he asked about Quincy. He said Quincy was an old friend. So I just told him where to find them both."

Parker thought for a moment. "I ran Janey out of town, but she's still operating in the territory southwest of here.

Quincy is an engineer, doing some type of land survey. I don't like the idea, but somehow he got official permission. He's working about seven miles northwest of here."

"Which trail did Hansen take?" O'Fallon asked.

The Indians on the porch pointed to the northwest.

O'Fallon untied the lead of his packhorse, tossed it to the boy holding the reins of Maria's horse. He turned his own horse and said, "Maria, can you stay here awhile? I think you can understand why I need to do this alone."

"We'll take care of her," Parker said.

She didn't object, but her dark eyes followed Sean as he raced out of the town.

When Jack Hansen arrived at the shanty, the tall grass around it was as red as if it were on fire. The cabin seemed deserted. The grass around it was barely grazed and the cabin itself showed few signs of being lived in.

Quincy was apparently not too far away, however. A mare that he used as a pack animal was still in the corral next to the cabin. Hansen let his black stallion into the corral with the other horse. The mare laid its ears back. Hansen grinned, and continued his search of the area.

The door to the cabin was latched with a wooden button. Its only window was boarded shut. Since there was no place to hide, Hansen decided to take the direct approach, and forced open the door. Inside, the building had no luxuries. In fact, it seemed little more than a storage shed. Its only furnishings were a small cot, a small wooden table with a new coal-oil lamp, a wooden chair. Writing pads and utensils were on the table. Some canvas packs were neatly stacked near the door.

By the fading light, Hansen went through the packs and found surveying equipment; rock, soil, and plant specimens; more blank pads and pencils; flour and beans; a handgun in a leather case. But Hansen did not find the package for which he had been sent. He returned everything to where he had found it, except for a few sourdough biscuits. He munched on these as he finished his search of the cabin.

A COLD, DARK TRAIL

Night birds called out in the distance. The wind whistling through the cracks in the door had a faint scent of winter. Hansen rolled a smoke and started his wait. He finally lit the lamp, placed it in the middle of the table, and settled back in the chair. He tilted it against the wall and rested his feet on the table.

It was not quite ten minutes later when Hansen heard the horse approaching. Hansen placed his feet firmly on the floor, lit another cigarette with the flame of the coal-oil lamp. Hansen heard Quincy talking to his packhorse in the corral, and then Quincy's footsteps approaching the door.

Quincy stepped briskly into the room. He was tall, round-faced, with a mustache. He removed his hat to reveal a balding head. He said, "Saw your horse outside. See you're making yourself comfortable. You're welcome to some supper, if you'd like, Mr.—"

Quincy spoke with a hint of an accent that Hansen could not identify.

"The name's Jack Hansen."

"Good evening to you, sir. I must say your presence is a surprise; I haven't had any visitors in the months I've been out here, and certainly expected none tonight."

Something about Quincy's attitude irritated Hansen. He said, "This isn't a social visit. You have something for me. A package."

Quincy frowned.

"A package, you say? I don't know of any package to be picked up. Who did you say sent you on this wild-goose chase?" He pulled out a cigar. "You have a light? Oh, no matter, I have in my pack—"

Hansen allowed Quincy to step over and reach toward his packs before he said, "Hold it."

The surveyor paused. He took the cigar from his mouth.

"Are you opposed to my smoking?"

"I'm opposed to you maybe trying to get that gun from your packs. Use the lamp."

"I really didn't feel like a smoke, anyway." He put the cigar back in its case.

"Look, Quincy, I've had a tough trip out here. I know you've been doing surveying work out here, and I want the notes and information you've gathered. Just give it to me and I'll be on my way."

Quincy crossed his arms in front of his chest.

"So you know about my assignment. That means you also work for Henry Simpson, or have some darned good intelligence. Unless you can produce proof that you also work for Simpson, you will get nothing from me."

Hansen slowly pulled one of the Smith & Wesson revolvers and lazily aimed it at Quincy's stomach.

"Have you ever seen a man gut-shot? He dies slowly, in agonizing pain. I'm going to kill you anyway, but wouldn't you rather it be quick and painless?" He took the cigarette from his mouth with his free hand. "But I would be glad to demonstrate the gut-shooting technique. Get me the package, however, and I'll be nice to you and kill you quickly."

"Listen, I don't know—"

The gunshot sounded like a cannon in the small room. The bullet grazed the inside of Quincy's thigh and hit the back wall. Quincy's face was white, but he was still standing. Hansen stepped toward Quincy and slammed his gun against the side of Quincy's face. Quincy fell to his knees.

"The package. Get the package. You have thirty seconds. The next time I won't miss, and you'll find yourself a helluva lot less of a man than you started."

Blood trickled down Quincy's face. He was slowly pushing himself up from the floor. Hansen could tell that Quincy was tensing, perhaps planning some kind of heroics.

"So you want to be a hard-nose? Guess you need another little lesson."

Hansen cocked the gun, casually took aim at Quincy's knee, when suddenly the door splintered behind him. He whirled, shot, but the bullet went wild as a rock-hard grip pulled him outside and slammed the pistol from his hand.

O'Fallon didn't even bother to read the sign; he just followed the trail used by Quincy when he came to town for his supplies. The horse was relatively rested, but O'Fallon urged the animal to even greater speed. He felt he had always been too late—to save Laura, to help Maria—and he felt sure that Hansen was going to kill the surveyor, Quincy.

The cabin came into view as the gunshot cracked and echoed through the evening air.

The horse galloped into the yard. O'Fallon dropped the reins as he jumped from the horse and kicked open the door.

Hansen held a cocked gun on a bloodied man, aimed at his kneecap. O'Fallon grabbed Hansen's throat and gun hand and pulled him through the door into the night. The gun went off harmlessly. O'Fallon pried it from the other man's grasp and tossed it into the weeds.

Hansen turned, furious.

"I don't know who the hell you are, but you've bit yourself off a passel of trouble—"

O'Fallon backhanded Hansen's face. His head snapped back, and he looked at O'Fallon in wide-eyed surprise.

"You! What are you doing here?" He rubbed his face. "It makes no difference. You're a dead man now."

He came off the ground in a flying leap that hit O'Fallon solidly in the stomach. The two fell to the ground and Hansen's hands were around the other man's neck. O'Fallon brought up a knee, which missed its target but caused Hansen to loosen his grip. Sean rolled to one side into the weeds.

The two men stood and warily circled each other.

"I don't know what you hope to accomplish," Hansen said through gritted teeth.

"I'm going to kill you, you son of a bitch," O'Fallon replied. "You're one of Culver's men, and that's reason enough. But after your little confession the other night, I have an even better reason."

Hansen paused, confused. O'Fallon used the opening. He struck out with a quick right and followed it with a left to the stomach. Hansen coughed, and stepped into O'Fallon with two quick jabs of his own. Sean grabbed the other man's arms and held them in a viselike grip. His face was just inches from Hansen's.

"Before you die, I want you to know your killer," O'Fallon said. "You were bragging about your victims the other night. What you didn't know is that one of those 'mountain bitches' was my wife. You and the rest of Culver's gang of thugs attacked, raped, and killed her and the rest of my family. I want Culver, but first I want you."

Something in O'Fallon's face hinted of madness, and for the first time in years Hansen became worried.

O'Fallon twisted, and threw Hansen against the wall. He lost his footing and his head crashed against the wood. He bounced off, tried to regain his balance, but somehow the Tennessee man was already on top of him. Sean took Hansen's head firmly in his hands and pounded it once, twice, three times against the wall. Bone crunched and blood spurted from the broken nose. O'Fallon lifted Hansen and threw him to the ground. Dust and weeds puffed around the gunfighter, lodging in the blood on his face, dripping to his shirt.

"It's easy to be tough with a gang behind you, or surprising an unarmed woman," O'Fallon said. "But a fair fight is a different matter, isn't it? Come on, you yellow bastard. This is for Laura, and Maria, and all your other victims. It won't bring them back, but it will keep you from killing any more."

Quincy, still dazed, stepped to the door. The darkness had covered the scene, but the stars gave enough light for Hansen to see O'Fallon. He seemed to be a blur, but Hansen once more pushed himself up and kicked at O'Fallon. The Tennessee man dodged, grabbed the foot, and twisted. He heard a loud pop and Hansen's scream as he hit the ground.

O'Fallon again picked up Hansen and repeatedly punched until his face was covered with bloody mud. Sean got a running start and threw the gunfighter through the remains of the door, barely missing Quincy. Hansen landed on his back. The splinters cut through his expensive clothes, tearing at his flesh, causing fresh blood to flow.

During the fight, O'Fallon had lost his gun. He saw it a few feet away, near the weeds. The gun in Hansen's left holster had miraculously not been jarred loose in the fight. Hansen was clearly illuminated by the kerosene lantern in the cabin. One eye was almost swollen shut, one leg was broken, but he still felt he was the better man with the gun—especially since he was the only one with a gun still holstered.

He spit out a tooth, smiled through the pain, and said, "Nice try, but you lose."

Hansen was quick and the revolver was a blur as it cleared the holster. But suddenly O'Fallon was gone. He had dived, rolled, picked up the Remington. He took several steps toward the cabin until he was almost in the door, cocked, and fired.

Two flashes of orange flame spit out in the night. Hansen's bullet kicked up dust, but O'Fallon's slug found its mark, hitting Hansen squarely in the chest, adding a new stream of red to the muddy shirt. Hansen fell backward, still holding onto his gun. O'Fallon shot again, this time hitting Hansen in the stomach.

Hansen fell, started to crawl toward the door.

O'Fallon watched Hansen pull himself along the floor, leaving a trail of blood behind him. He grabbed the table, tried to pull himself up. He had not let go of his revolver.

The kerosene lamp continued to burn brightly. Sean hesitated briefly, but then Hansen again cocked his gun to take aim. O'Fallon's gun blazed again. This time the shot hit the lamp, shattering the glass. Flames spread down the table and along the floor.

Hansen saw the fire coming toward him. His eyes grew wide in terror. He screamed, and shot wildly.

O'Fallon shot twice more. The bullets hit, and Hansen collapsed into the flames, which were now snaking up the walls.

Chapter 9

The fire quickly spread. O'Fallon thought at first he might have heard more screams. Quincy stumbled toward the burning building, as if he were going to try and pull Hansen from the flames. O'Fallon reached out to stop him, but Quincy said, "My bags."

O'Fallon pulled his hand away.

Now that it was over, O'Fallon felt drained. He stood and watched as Quincy grabbed his packs, and dragged them through the door. The canvas was smoking in places. Quincy removed his jacket and hit the smoldering spots to keep them from also bursting into flame.

The flames started to lick at the roof.

The building, though small, burned brightly. It suddenly shot up in flames, reaching toward the clouds, lighting the night sky. The smell of burned flesh was strong. The heat was more intense than Sean would have thought. It pushed against the two men, and it seemed at first that O'Fallon would try to stand against the forces.

"Come on, man, you're going to get killed!" Quincy said.

When O'Fallon finally moved, however, it was more because of the horses in the pole corral than Quincy. The animals were panicky, pushing against the poles, when Sean ran over to the gate. The stallion was kicking and running crazily, but O'Fallon slipped between the kicks, grabbed hold of the animal's neck, and said with a surprisingly gentle voice, "Just take it easy, boy . . . you're okay . . . easy . . ."

Quincy dropped his jacket on his packs, ran over to help Sean, but O'Fallon needed no help. He was leading the stallion away from the fire. O'Fallon's horses were following him in single file, but Quincy's horse bolted and ran.

Shots suddenly rang out. O'Fallon said, more to the horses than to Quincy, "Don't worry . . . it's only Hansen's gun and bullets exploding from the heat."

Sean felt tired. He watched the fire for a few minutes longer before Quincy said, "How can you be so calm? You just killed a man, and were almost killed yourself!"

"He got what he deserved. He recently raped and knifed a woman. He was one of a bunch that raped and killed my wife. He would have killed you and me for the fun of it, if he had gotten the chance." O'Fallon paused, then added, "Better tend to your own livestock. I think they took off in that direction." He then led his horses further from the fire as Quincy muttered to himself and took off after his own animals.

Finally left alone, O'Fallon breathed deeply, trying to clear his head. The air was bitter and burned his lungs. He had intended to kill Hansen, and had succeeded. The gunfighter had suffered before he died. But O'Fallon was not feeling vindicated.

The flames started to die down. Bits of ash floated toward the sky like dirty snow. In a few places, the hot ashes caused the grass to smolder, and O'Fallon realized his moment of vengeance threatened to start a fire he could never put out. He felt vaguely sick as he walked through the grass, stamping out the smoky patches. The few pieces left of the structure caved in, sending up a shower of ash and dust. The dark edged in again. Soon, only a faint orange appeared in patches on the ground.

O'Fallon tied the horses away from the flaming cabin, then sat, nearly motionless, watching the orange coals darken and the smoke thin. O'Fallon heard Quincy approaching from behind in the darkness. He was muttering, "Damned critters, almost got away from me. . . ." Quincy stopped suddenly. O'Fallon reached for his pipe, but it had fallen from his pocket sometime during the fight.

"What are you doing?" Quincy asked.

"Waiting for the fire to die down enough that I can get the body."

"And then what?"

Sean didn't bother to answer. Quincy tied his horse and sat down beside O'Fallon.

"I'd like to thank you for showing up when you did. Another few minutes, and I probably would have been dead. You've been trailing Hansen for long?"

O'Fallon glanced at Quincy. He was still pale, but seemed in control of himself.

"Long enough. It was just luck that I found him when I did. He had been a renegade during the war, and I was really hoping he would lead me to the man that had been his leader. I didn't expect the trail to stop here."

"You didn't have any choice in the matter, Mr.—"

"Sean O'Fallon."

"Josiah Quincy."

"Hansen would have killed you after he got what he was after," O'Fallon continued. "At the risk of being rude, what makes you so important that you would have to be killed?"

The two men stared into the burned remains of the cabin. Quincy pulled out a cigar, but did not light it.

"I'll lay my cards on the table," Quincy said. "My assignment here was supposed to be confidential, but apparently word of it somehow leaked out. Besides, the least I can do is give you some information, after you saved my life." He tapped the end of the cigar on his leg and continued, "I work for Henry Simpson, an Eastern railroad and land developer. I've been checking out the land for rail routes, mining potential, and so on. It may be years before this territory is officially opened to the white men, but Mr. Simpson believes in being prepared. Information like this is difficult to come by since the Indian leaders have officially allowed very few of these studies."

"So Hansen was hired to steal your information and kill you before anybody else could get it."

Now the chilly night air was moving in, blowing away some of the stench from the fire.

"It's the only thing that makes sense. Information is power, and those who have the best information can better plan for railroad expansion and land development. But Simpson, like all rich and powerful men, has a lot of enemies. Who do you think Hansen was working for?"

"My guess is Winston Culver. Hansen rode with Culver during the war, and I suspect he could still be one of Culver's men."

"I vaguely remember hearing the name during the war. But I don't remember Culver being mentioned as one of Simpson's rivals."

"Then maybe I was following a dead-end trail. It wouldn't be the first time."

O'Fallon stood and approached the ruins. He could feel the heat through the soles of his boots. Sean kicked through the debris until he found the specific pile of rubble he was seeking. He tossed to one side a chunk of blackened wood to reveal what was left of Jack Hansen, gunfighter, former Culver's Raider.

The body was burned beyond recognition. It no longer had a face; the arms and legs were fused to the body; the skin had blackened into a solid mass. O'Fallon kicked away some more ashes and laid a canvas from his packs on the ground. He rolled the body onto the canvas and started to wrap the material around the charred flesh.

Quincy, surprised, said, "What the hell! What are you doing?"

"I'm getting the body ready for delivery."

"Delivery? What are you talking about?"

"I'm bringing Hansen back to Parkersburg."

"Why? The wisest thing for you might be to stop while you're ahead. You managed to beat Hansen, but he was just one man. Anybody with the resources to determine the nature of my work—down to my very location—is obviously very powerful. And apparently he wouldn't think twice of using murder to achieve his ends. Next time there might not be just one man, and you might not walk away."

O'Fallon shrugged and said, "Maybe Hansen wasn't working for Culver. And maybe he was. He's still the only lead I have. Maybe I can goad Hansen's boss—whoever it is—into the open. I'll take my chances."

Quincy stood and lit his cigar. O'Fallon handed Quincy the end of a rope to tie the canvas.

"What's your next move?"

"I want Culver to know I'm after him. I want him and his men to know I'm the one that killed Hansen. So I'm going to drop the body off at Parkersburg, where the message will be plain when the others come looking for him."

O'Fallon saddled the stallion. He tied the canvas-covered body across the horse's saddle and turned to his own mount. Quincy looked thoughtful as he started to prepare his own horses.

"Mind if I ride along? I'm headed for Parkersburg, too. I've stored most of my notes and such there and need to pick them up, before heading back to Chicago."

"Suit yourself."

The two rode in silence. Sean was weary. Leading the grisly body on the nervous stallion made the trip seem endless. The predawn breeze carried with it a trace of cold dampness. If he closed his eyes, O'Fallon could almost imagine he was home. But then the breeze shifted, carrying with it the smell of charred flesh, and O'Fallon realized again that he had no home.

The strange parade crested a hill as the sun moved above the horizon. In the distance, the small town of Parkersburg could be seen. Some of the townspeople were already up, preparing for the day. After a slight hesitation, O'Fallon changed directions. He would not ride past the school. This parade was no sight for children.

Still, somebody spotted O'Fallon's group while they were far away and spread the word. A crowd was waiting by the time O'Fallon rode up to Parker's store. Parker stepped onto the porch, followed by Maria. The woman ran to the edge of the porch, and smiled in relief. Then she saw the body on the stallion and the smile froze on her face.

O'Fallon had a sudden yearning to be with Maria again as they had been on the trail, a few days before, when her head rested on his shoulder and he had felt an unfamiliar warmth. Now, he again felt cold.

"You made it a lot faster than I thought," Parker said. "But, then, some of us figured you wouldn't come back at all. Some of us wish you hadn't made it back—at least not with this. Couldn't you have buried it in the hills or something?"

O'Fallon loosened the ropes that held the body. It slid to the ground and hit with a sickening thud.

"Here's Jack Hansen, the terrible gunfighter," O'Fallon said. "Or what's left of him. He won't be raping or killing any more women."

Parker said, "I had no liking for Hansen, especially after what he did to Maria, but my god—"

"Hansen was trying to kill me when O'Fallon came on the scene," Quincy interrupted. "The two of them were in a fair fight. The burning was an accident."

O'Fallon took out his pocketknife and cut open the canvas. The crowd gasped, but Parker said, "There was no need for that."

Maria stepped off the porch and walked over to the burned body. She looked at it, as if to reassure herself that Hansen was in fact dead, and suddenly started sobbing. She reached out to O'Fallon and buried her face in his chest.

"It wasn't just Maria. Hansen was one of the Culver's Raiders that killed my wife. I'm now going after Culver, and I plan to do the same—or worse—to him. When his men come out to find out what happened to Hansen, I want them to see this sight and report back to Culver that his days are numbered."

The crowd rumbled again, whether in agreement or disagreement O'Fallon neither knew nor cared. He figured that, one way or another, Culver would learn about this incident.

A boy appeared around the side of the building leading O'Fallon's packhorse. One of the older men grabbed the reins and ordered the boy back around the building. The man led the packed horse and handed the reins to O'Fallon. Maria looked up at Sean's impassive face, squeezed his arm, and went back inside. O'Fallon wanted to follow her, but forced himself to remain standing. Parker was now talking again.

"I'm grateful to you for helping Maria, but I think it might be best for all concerned if you just kind of rode out of here," Parker said. "We have enough problems without you involving us in your fight."

O'Fallon looked toward the interior of the store, but said nothing in reply. He mounted his own horse and rode east. The rising sun cast a shadow behind him.

Parker spit off the porch.

"He's as bad as Hansen," Parker said. "We don't need his kind out here. There's no excuse for burning a man alive."

The crowd started to gather around Hansen's corpse, talking about it in hushed tones.

Maria stepped back through the door. She had washed the tears from her face, but looked very tired.

"Don't be so quick to judge," she said, softly. "Hansen probably got off easy. Sean's a good man."

Quincy said, "O'Fallon would be a good man to have on our side."

"On your side," Parker said. "You're one of Simpson's agents, but I'm trying to stay neutral in this thing. I did agree to keep your information in my safe, but even that was against my better judgment. Now there are only a few fighting to take our land away from us; soon, there will be many. I don't want to help anybody move us off our land again."

"Like we've talked about before, Parker, that isn't possible in this modern world. You can't stop progress; the railroads will be here in a few years, like it or not. You had best side with those that can help you at least keep some of the pie, or you'll lose it all."

Parker abruptly turned and stepped inside.

"How about you, Maria?" Quincy said.

"I learned a long time ago we can never remain neutral in the wars of the white men. My husband was killed because he tried. It is not a mistake I intend to repeat."

"Which means?"

"It comes to the lesser of many evils. I don't trust your Mr. Simpson. But I know that others, such as Sean's enemy, can be far worse. I admire Sean, and will help him. If that also means helping you and Simpson, then that is my choice." She looked down the street, past the crowd. "Are you going to try and recruit Sean? Or are you going to leave him out of it?"

"He doesn't know it yet," Quincy said, "but he's already involved."

"I thought so. Tell me how I can help."

"Since the first attempt to get the information failed, I'm pretty sure another attempt will be made, probably before I can even get to New Hope. Next time I may not be so lucky. Now, if I could find somebody I could trust to deliver the package for me, and if that somebody would not be an obvious choice . . ."

"I understand. I'll help you. Let's go inside and talk."

Quincy followed Maria into Parker's store.

The voices from the crowd at Parker's store blurred into a muttering, and then gave way to the early morning wind as O'Fallon rode into the rising sun. The bright light was harsh, but dark clouds that promised rain were on the horizon. O'Fallon pulled the brim of his stained and battered Stetson down on his forehead, to shade his eyes.

The sun rose slowly. An occasional cloud cast a brief shadow, and the wind blew damp and cold.

O'Fallon looked around him as he considered his next move.

In spite of what Quincy had said, Sean was sure Hansen had been working for Culver up to the end. O'Fallon reasoned that if Quincy's engineering survey information was important enough to kill for, Culver would not give up just because the first attempt failed. The logical move would be to trail Quincy until Culver made his next move.

O'Fallon was now alone. He turned off the trail to find higher ground, where he could watch Quincy from the distance.

Chapter 10

Michael Braddock personally met with the Indian at an old abandoned farmhouse, about ten miles northwest of New Hope, less than twenty-four hours after O'Fallon had left Parkersburg.

"This had better be good, Lancer," Braddock said.

"I thought you might want to know about this," the Indian said. He was tall, dirty, and dressed in patched clothes. He was young, but he was not going to be intimidated by the fat man. Lancer continued coolly, "The stranger's name is Sean O'Fallon. He killed Hansen." When Braddock didn't answer right away, Lancer continued, "O'Fallon apparently beat Hansen, shot him, and then burned him alive."

Braddock scowled. Culver should have listened to him and cut Hansen from the payroll long ago. Braddock had always felt Hansen was an egotistical incompetent, good only for the simplest assignments. But what could be simpler than getting the information from Quincy and then killing the man? Still, even when he gave Hansen the assignment in the hotel bar a few days ago, he had some doubts about Hansen's ability to carry through. Those doubts were now vindicated.

"What else?"

"Not much. He threatened to kill somebody named Culver. You know the man?" Braddock ignored the question, and the Indian continued, "You said you wanted to know about anything unusual happening in the nation. Everybody knows you're interested in the territory, so I put two and two together and . . . well, I figured that even if Hansen wasn't working for you, this information might be worth a few dollars. And apparently you do feel it's important, or you wouldn't be here."

Braddock liked the looks of this Indian. As a boy, Lancer had started out as a simple informant, but had grown into a genuinely tough man. Unlike Hansen, he was smart, and might prove valuable to the organization. Braddock said, "This man that killed Hansen . . . Do you think he's really that tough? Or was he just lucky?"

"Didn't look that tough to me," the Indian answered. "He didn't act or talk like a bad man with a gun. If anything, he seemed a little crazy."

Braddock and the Indian were meeting in the yard in front of an abandoned house. Braddock leaned against the buggy that he had ridden from town.

"Where is O'Fallon now?"

"After he threatened to kill Culver, he just up and rode away. I didn't see any sign of him on the way in. I imagine he's long gone."

"Did he take anything with him? Did the surveyor give him any kind of package?"

"Not that I could tell. He just up and left. But, then, Parker kind of encouraged the leaving. You know how he is with strangers."

"Yes. I remember from my days with the Indian bureau that he was a difficult man to deal with."

Braddock tapped his fingers on the wooden seat of the buggy. His first thought was that the stranger was working for Simpson, and had been sent out as a bodyguard to ensure the safe return of the engineer and his information. But O'Fallon's subsequent actions didn't fit that idea. O'Fallon had left the surveyor again by himself, with a lot of miles between the Cherokee Nation and New Hope. So maybe there was still a chance to salvage this operation.

"You've done well. How would you like a more important job?" Braddock asked.

"Sure. Name it."

"Your instincts were right; Hansen was working for me. Now, I want you and a few of your friends to finish the job that Hansen botched. You have any problems with that?"

The Indian showed dark teeth in a cruel smile.

"Good," Braddock said. "As you know, a survey has been conducted over this past summer by an engineer named Josiah Quincy. What I want are the notes and records that Quincy made in his survey. If he's hidden the information, find out where it is and get it." He paused, thinking, then added, "No, I have a better idea. I want to know *everything* he has managed to find out about the territory, and much of it may not be written down. If he has the notes on him, go ahead and get them, but don't settle for that. Make him talk; make him tell you everything there is to know. That may take awhile." Braddock's fingers continued to tap the buggy seat as he planned. "Bring him here for questioning. I foreclosed on this property quite awhile back, so you'll have plenty of privacy for the job. I'll send somebody up here to record the results of your . . . inquiry. I don't care how you make him talk; I'm sure an intelligent young buck like yourself can come up with some clever ways to obtain the information. And when you're through, I don't want him to be able to make another survey or to talk to anybody else, ever again. You understand me?"

"I know a man that's just right for the job. He enjoys that kind of work. He could get information out of a fence post."

"Good. Remember to keep it simple. Report back to me as soon as possible."

"What about that stranger that killed Hansen?"

"I think you're right. He probably got lucky. Still, it might be a good idea to keep a watch for him, just in case. If you run across him, do with him as you will. It's no concern of mine."

A cold rain had been falling for two days and nights, dripping down Lancer's long hair in a greasy stream. Bridger, a head taller than Lancer, and another Indian named Oxman were huddled together in the darkness, oblivious of the rain. A fourth man held the reins of the horses, slightly apart from the circle.

"What'd you find, Lance?" Oxman asked.

"Quincy's down in the next hollow, trying to keep a little fire going. He's being followed by another man. I suspect it's the one that made the fuss back at Parker's."

"They're not together? They rode into town at the same time."

Lancer shrugged. The other Indians saw the slight movement in spite of the darkness.

"Who knows? Who cares? Braddock said don't worry about him, but I think he might want to cause us trouble. Let's give him something to think about before we pick up Quincy for . . . questioning. You know the plan . . . bring him to the abandoned farm I told you about. Bridger, your job is to soften him up. Braddock's sending a man to help with the questioning. So don't rough him up too bad at first."

The men were speaking in whispers. Their voices could barely be heard in the rain. Oxman creased his forehead, made a nervous movement with his hand.

"No problem with me, Lance, but why do we want to mess with this other dude? Maybe we should just do the job we're being paid to do."

"Scared?" Bridger sneered.

"Just seems like wasted effort, is all."

"I say let's teach the prick to stay out of our way in case he gets any bright ideas," Bridger said.

Lancer smiled. "They both should be asleep soon, and we'll make our moves. Any more discussion?" The steady sound of raindrops hitting the ground could be heard, but no more voices. "Good. Leave your horses here. No use giving them advance warning."

The cold rain had chilled O'Fallon to the bone. In spite of the bad weather, Quincy had made good time; he made no attempt to hide his trail, and O'Fallon had no difficulty following the engineer.

A COLD, DARK TRAIL

So far, Quincy had apparently not suspected he was being followed. He had camped in the open and, with difficulty, started a small, sputtering fire during a lull in the storm. The rain had started again, however, and threatened to extinguish the small flame. O'Fallon, certain that Quincy would stay put until morning, camped far enough away that he could also build a small fire without being detected. He had quickly erected a canvas lean-to, which helped keep out some of the rain and protect the fire. He was far from comfortable, but was in better shape than Quincy.

The two were now close to New Hope, Missouri, near the Indian Territory border. O'Fallon figured Quincy would catch one of the trains at New Hope and head back East to personally deliver the information he had gathered. It seemed strange to O'Fallon that men would kill for a few numbers on paper, but he knew that if the territory ever opened up, such information would be invaluable. It could help determine railroad routes, town sites, maybe even locations for mineral excavations. Sean was a little disappointed that the trip so far had been uneventful. He had hoped Quincy might attract another of Culver's lackeys, and this time O'Fallon would make sure to get some current information about Culver. He hadn't intended to kill Hansen so quickly; but what choice had there been?

O'Fallon warmed his hands around the steaming coffee cup. The rain streamed from the canvas stretched a few inches above his head. He moved his legs to try and get more comfortable, and thought about Maria. It had been pleasant to talk with her and to hold her. O'Fallon wondered, however, what the woman could see in him, even if he was free? She had been married to an important man in her nation. She had received a good education. She had a home, with friends who cared about her. O'Fallon, on the other hand, felt he had nothing. He had lost his home and his dreams years before. Now, his only goal was to avenge his wife before he died.

O'Fallon realized he was gripping the coffee cup so tightly that his knuckles were white. He forced himself to calm down, and tried to put the thoughts out of his head. Still, the familiar memories haunted him, as he thought about that evening in May 1866, when he returned home for the last time.

O'Fallon had walked painfully over the once-familiar woods and hills. The leaves were a pale green and light lay in splotches on the ground. Home was only three ridges away, and he was anxious to get there.

Yet, the pain forced him to go slowly. The sights and sounds pressed upon him with great force.

The small, slow-running creek.

The old oak, where he used to run and jump and play.

The hill where he had first kissed Laura.

Sean shook his head sadly. So many changes had occurred. How many more would there be? It was a question he didn't want to think about. He had sent letters, but they were never answered. And if letters had been sent from home, they had somehow gotten lost in transit. Still, Sean knew Laura would be waiting for him, even after more than two years.

So why wasn't his step lighter? Why wasn't he smiling at the thought of finally returning home?

Sean was wearing simple clothes, now worn thin from the long walk from the St. Louis convalescent home. He was carrying his few possessions in a leather bag and was wearing a Remington revolver. He'd had to use it twice already against would-be thieves, and he would be glad to get home where he could put up the gun and return to a life of farming. He was tired of killing, and wanted to get on with his life with Laura. He was looking forward to starting his family.

He walked slowly, growing more uneasy with each step.

The ridges of his home had never been heavily populated, but there had always been people. Yet, all he had seen for the past several miles were burned-out farms, poorly tended fields, and people who would not look him in the eye.

A cardinal flew by him in the sunlight, into the shadows

of the trees, and Sean picked up his pace. Only one more ridge to go, and he would be home.

Sean crossed the final ridge, and found his unspoken fears fulfilled. The sun was still shining, but for a minute he was lost in darkness. He opened his eyes, but the scene before him remained unchanged.

A blackened outline on the ground indicated where the cabin had once stood.

Dark and waxy green vines were creeping along the burnt ground.

A few small weeds and sprouts, with at least two seasons' growth, had invaded the edge of the blackness.

The pole barn was still standing, but the weeds there were as tall as a man.

Birds flitted about the shrubs and barn, but no humans or livestock could be seen.

Sean started slowly down the hill, along a familiar path now overgrown with weeds. He stopped at the root cellar, noted that no food had been left and that the floor was littered with broken jars and rat droppings.

It seemed like a dream, even more unreal than any of the battles, the town raids, even the army hospital. In those instances, the strangeness was expected, for he was in new situations and places he had never seen before. But this was his home. What had been his home.

He stepped to the edge of the black. It crunched beneath his feet. He kicked it with his toe. The rain had settled the ashes, and much of it had mixed with the soil underneath to form a hard, rocklike mass.

He walked over to the pile of stones that had been a fireplace. Smaller piles of charred wood indicated where his parents' room had been, the room where he and his brother had slept, and the section that he, his brother, and his father had built for Laura. Sean remembered how his family had promised to look after her while he was away, and the plans to build their own cabin when he returned.

Where the new section stood was not as charred as the

rest, since some of the wood had still been a little green and had not burned as quickly.

Laura, of course, would probably now be staying at her parents' house. Even though they might still have been angry about the marriage, they would not reject her in a time of need. She would, of course, still be there, waiting for him.

A bit of reflected sunlight caught his eye: a sparkle in a bunch of weeds covering a small pile of debris. Sean got on his knees, sifted through the black dirt, not sure what he was looking for.

He found a button to one of Laura's dresses. Shadows seemed to cross before his eyes, and he clutched the button tightly.

The button was from the dress she had been wearing on their wedding day.

Sean dug some more, found another button, and then a tarnished silver locket.

The weed-covered pile remained. Sean pulled up a hand full of green, tossed it to one side. It came up easily, for the roots were shallow in the ground. He pulled up another bunch, and this one had a tangle of cloth in the roots.

Gently, tenderly, Sean removed the dirt and pulled the rest of the material from the ground. It was the dress she had worn on their wedding day. It was in tatters, and was starting to rot from being so long in the ground.

He widened his search, and found one of her night dresses—the one she had worn on their wedding night. He clutched the muddy cloth tightly in his hand. He rocked back and forth, wanting to cry. The thought of seeing Laura again, of being with her again, had allowed Sean to survive, and to learn to walk again. But if she was gone . . .

He rose with some difficulty, but still did not move from the spot. He spread the damp material on the fireplace stones, rubbed his eyes.

Suddenly, Sean felt a presence. His hand moved to the Remington and he looked carefully around him.

A gaunt figure, several years younger than Sean, stepped out from behind the old barn.

A COLD, DARK TRAIL

"Welcome home, Sean."

His brother's voice was dull, as were his eyes. Sean had anticipated bear hugs and wrestling matches at his homecoming, but Ian made no attempt to come any closer.

"I heard you were coming home," Ian said. "Word still travels fast in these hills."

"Then why didn't you come to greet me?"

Ian shrugged, gestured at the ruins of the cabin. "How could I tell you about this? There is no way."

"It would have been better than my finding out like this."

"Don't be angry with me."

Sean wanted to shake his brother, but did nothing. Sean was keeping his emotions tightly under control.

"When did this happen?" he asked.

"About two months after you left."

"What happened?"

Ian shrugged. Sean moved quickly, forgetting his painful leg. Ian didn't seem surprised to see his brother coming at him; his blank expression didn't change. Sean slapped his brother once, twice. Ian's eyes opened wide, and then he collapsed in Sean's arms. Ian cried, the sobs racking his body. Sean wanted to cry, as well, but could not. He held his brother, but said nothing. He knew that whatever he could say would be silly and empty.

Finally, Ian choked out, "We tried to stop them. We really, truly, tried to stop them."

"Where is everybody? Where is Laura?"

Ian sobbed even harder. The sounds were harsh and ugly. When he finally got himself under control again, he pulled back and said, "I'm sorry, Sean. I should have met you on the road. This is one hell of a homecoming."

O'Fallon glanced at the tattered rags on the fireplace stones.

"Tell me what happened. Tell me about Laura."

Ian looked away.

"Don't judge me, Sean. . . ."

"Just tell me what happened."

"They came in the night, without warning. Nobody even

knew they were operating in this part of the country." Ian's voice was dull, lifeless. "Still, they came. A dozen, two dozen. Nobody can ever know for sure. There were a bunch of local boys, and some that were strangers. They were renegades, led by a Winston Culver."

"Who were the local boys?"

"Pig-Eye Smith, Lon Cunningham, a few others. They came in the night. Dad and me, we grabbed our guns, but it was too late. Too late."

A frog jumped into the blackened square. Sean nudged it with his toe. Surprised, the frog jumped back into the bushes.

"There were too many of them," Ian continued. "I shot one, Dad got two, but then they got him. Mom killed one before they got her."

"You all did your best."

"You're not angry at me?"

"No. Go ahead. What happened then?"

"I took a slug in the shoulder, which knocked me out. When I woke, three days later, I found myself in the gully behind the barn. I was feverish, and wandered around for another day before the Scarry boys found me. By then it was too late. The Culver bunch was gone."

"Laura." Sean's voice was a whisper. "Tell me what happened to Laura." Ian choked again. "For God's sake, man, it wasn't your fault. I must know what happened to my wife."

Ian pointed up the hill, past where the house used to be, to the small family cemetery. Ian leaned against the barn as Sean took slow strides up the hill.

The graves were not new. The tops had sunk in, and needed filling. Other signs of neglect were also apparent. More tall weeds, tilted markers. One wooden plank had been simply marked:

Laura O'Fallon
1848–1865

Sean stood for long minutes at the grave site. His vision was blurred and dark, and he felt an unfamiliar cold. He clutched the silver locket in his hand and said, "Laura, I vow to you to avenge your death. I won't rest until I find Culver, and kill him and as many of his men as I can find. This I swear to you."

The sun continued to burn brightly, but Sean no longer noticed. He walked back down the hill as if in a dream and said, "Tell me everything. I know you well enough to know you're holding something back."

"I can't."

"Dammit, tell me!"

Ian hugged the old barn, as if it might provide him support.

"I don't know the details. I pieced together what I could. Laura apparently put up a good fight, but she was outnumbered. Apparently most of them . . . had their way with her. Many times."

"Why didn't somebody help?"

"A lot of others were also burned out. Most people were hiding or trying to protect themselves. Everybody was scared. But I should have been able to stop them. When I failed you, I failed all of us. . . ."

"And the house?"

"I swear, Sean, I didn't look at her. When I returned, even feverish, I knew what I had to do. They left her body, naked, where it fell, and I covered her as best I could."

"The house, Ian. What about the house?"

"I got Mrs. Scarry to help with Laura. I found the bodies of Mom and Dad in the gully, near where I had been thrown, as well. And then I buried them all." He rubbed his eyes. "You have to understand how it was. Everything in the house was broken, and soiled, and used, and dirty. I could not get the image of Laura, bloody and dirty and naked under the blanket, out of my head." He looked up at Sean. "Don't judge me. I did what I had to do."

"Go on."

"After they were buried, I walked through the ruins of the house, saw where they had eaten our food, used the front room as an outhouse. And I saw Laura's clothes, dirty and

torn and scattered on the floor, and on your old bed. . . . ''
He took a deep breath, and continued, ''I burned the house.
I couldn't stand the dirt, the filth, of being reminded of . . .
that. So I burned the house. To cleanse it.'' He looked up
again. ''Can you understand, Sean? Can you?''

''Yes.''

''You and me are the only ones left. I'm living on the
Shaughnessy place, now. I do work for them.''

''Are Pig-Eye, Cunningham, still in the area?''

''Yes.''

''And the strangers?''

''Gone. Nobody knows where.''

Sean reached into his bag, pulled out a silver dollar, placed
it in Ian's hand, and said, ''This is all I have, but you are
welcome to it. I have some business to tend to, and I doubt
if I'll ever be back. Sell the farm. Go someplace new. Start
over again.'' Ian's eyes were haunted. ''I don't judge you.
You did the right thing.''

Sean had started to walk away, when Ian called out.

''One more thing . . . you need to know. We think . . .
Laura was with your child when she died.''

Sean paused for only a second before starting toward the
Cunningham place.

Chapter 11

O'Fallon woke to the sound of rain, and of something more. The noise had been slight, and might have been only his horses moving at the end of their lines. O'Fallon, however, trusted his instincts, and something seemed out of place. He listened carefully, but all he could hear now was rain hitting the canvas overhead and the puddles outside his makeshift shelter. Sean pulled his Remington and placed his good leg under him. He moved cautiously, without sound.

Suddenly, two shadows materialized out of the rain and the canvas collapsed around O'Fallon. He felt the weight of a heavy man on top of the wet canvas on his back. O'Fallon struck out with a fist, felt it hit solid muscle and bone. The figure on top of him let out a grunt. O'Fallon pushed the figure away and tried to roll to the ground.

The material twisted around him and the other figures moved in. Strong hands grabbed him from behind, but O'Fallon twisted free and backhanded the attacker with his revolver.

Still trying to free himself, he rolled and fired at the second of the men, who dived behind a small bush. It was little protection, but it would perhaps hide him in the darkness.

Sean was now coated with cold, slippery mud, but finally freed himself from the canvas. He put weight on his good leg and jumped toward the third figure. Sean hit the man solidly with his shoulder, and his opponent fell backward, pumping his feet under him, trying to keep his balance. He fell against the horses, which caused them to panic. One lunged against its rope until it broke.

The man behind the bush jumped up and ran toward O'Fallon. The two men went down, but the other man flipped Sean over. O'Fallon tried to land on his back, but was off balance and hit on his bad leg.

The pain shot through him, taking his breath away. It stopped him only for a second, but was long enough. He felt the blow to the back of his head. He fell, cursed himself for letting his attackers sneak up on him under cover of the rain.

A wet, muddy boot kicked the gun from his hand, and then kicked again. O'Fallon managed to twist enough that the boot missed his leg, but he took the kick in his chest, knocking the breath out of him again. Strong hands pulled him to his feet, held him in a viselike grip. The taller of the three pulled off O'Fallon's hat, letting the rain stream down his face and under his collar. Their faces were partially hidden by the rain, but O'Fallon could tell they were Indians; he would be able to recognize them again.

"So this is the tough guy that killed Hansen?" the taller one said. "Don't look so tough now." He punched O'Fallon in the stomach.

A man with greasy black hair pulled Sean up and said, "You're pretty slick." His face was just inches from O'Fallon's. He spoke in a voice so low that the others couldn't hear. "You leave damned little trail. If I hadn't been looking for you, I probably never would have found you. You're pretty good. But I'm better. I just wanted you to know that." He laughed, then hit O'Fallon again on the side of the head. "I think you understand me now. I'm better than you. And if you show your face again, I'll kill you."

The black-haired man threw O'Fallon into the mud. He said, "You all go ahead and pick up Quincy. I'll report to Braddock and join you later."

O'Fallon moved slightly, rippling the shallow, muddy water, and groaned in spite of himself. He tried to push himself off the ground. Lancer kicked. The point of his boot hit

O'Fallon on the chin. The darkness overtook him as he collapsed in the mud.

Sean woke cold, wet, and with the taste of mud in his mouth. He painfully lifted his head from the puddle near the crumpled canvas that had formed his shelter. The sky was lighter in the east, and the rain was still coming down. It had lessened some, but could still wash out any sign that his attackers might have left behind. He would have to act fast to catch up with them.

He moved slowly, however, pushing himself out of the water as best he could, to sit against a tree. His horses were gone. He stood, struggling to his feet with the help of the tree, and walked painfully to the stream, about a quarter mile away. He had camped far enough away, on high ground, so that he would not be flooded if the creek rose because of the rain. It had now swollen to the top of its banks. The rain had washed gullies from the sides of the stream, muddying the water.

He walked upstream to where he remembered seeing a rock outcropping. It provided no shelter, but did form a shallow pool where clear water would have collected. O'Fallon thrust his face into the water, and moved it slowly back and forth to remove the grit. He rinsed out his mouth with fresh water.

He tenderly felt his face and his side. Apparently neither his jaw nor his ribs were broken. His leg was sore, but still not as bad as it had been in the months of his hospitalization, and then during his recovery. He could live with the pain.

O'Fallon cleaned himself the best he could, took a deep breath, and retraced his steps back to the ransacked camp.

He found his hat and his gun where they had fallen. The mud where the horses had been tied had been torn up, where the animals had apparently been startled by the attackers. A piece of broken lead rope remained tied to the tree where the saddle horse had gotten away before the Indians could get to it. Still, they had taken O'Fallon's supplies and his packhorse, though they had left the saddle. He pulled the canvas up from the ground to reveal his saddlebags, with the spare box of cartridges, his money, and his few personal items.

He threw the saddlebags over his shoulder, and started toward Quincy's camp. O'Fallon knew he had been unconscious for too long; by now, the Indians would have Quincy and a long lead. When he arrived at Quincy's camp, the fire had long been burned out and the trail had almost been obliterated by the rain. O'Fallon searched the ground in everwidening circles, and came upon fresh horse tracks. He followed the tracks for almost two hours before O'Fallon was able to find his horse. He led it back to his camp, where he could saddle it and start on the Indians' trail.

The sky was now gray, and the rain had finally stopped for a few moments. More dark clouds were in the distance, and O'Fallon knew another storm would hit before the day was over. He would have at least a few hours of clear weather.

The rain had washed out some of the sign, and another heavy rain could destroy the rest. For now, however, the tracks were relatively clear.

In the early afternoon O'Fallon came to a fork in the trail. He stepped off his horse to examine the ground.

Most of the tracks led toward the northeast. A single set led to the east.

O'Fallon walked slowly, trying to loosen up his leg, as he tried to decide what to do next.

Even though O'Fallon had been almost unconscious, he had heard enough to guess the rest. Culver, or whoever was after Quincy's information, was no longer content with just his notes. Now they wanted everything that Quincy knew about the territory. O'Fallon knew that the Indians would not hesitate to torture the engineer to convince him to provide the information, if need be. And they would most certainly kill him. O'Fallon knew he should try to rescue Quincy, if he could. If he did not, Quincy would surely die.

The single set of tracks broke off from the others and headed toward New Hope. O'Fallon also knew one of the Indians was going to report to his boss, probably in New Hope. That person could be Culver. Culver's name had not

A COLD, DARK TRAIL   101

been mentioned. Instead, it was somebody named Braddock. But Culver could be working under a false name these days. Or it could be that Braddock, like Hansen, was working for Culver. In any case, it could be the lead that O'Fallon had been looking for.

Thunder boomed in the distance. Black clouds rolled overhead and the first large drop hit the muddy ground around O'Fallon.

He had a choice. He could follow the tracks to where Quincy had been taken prisoner, or he could follow the tracks that might lead to Culver. O'Fallon looked into the sky as the next several drops hit him in the eyes.

He thought, What is Quincy to me? I saved his hide once. Is he worth losing my best—possibly my only—lead to Culver?

Thunder boomed and the rain started to fall heavily as O'Fallon stiffly mounted his horse and headed to New Hope.

The remaining miles passed quickly, in spite of the heavy rain. O'Fallon moved with greater urgency, pushing the horse as fast as it could go under the miserable conditions. The downpour soon destroyed any traces left by the Indian's passage, so Sean stopped trying to track the Indian and made a straight shot to New Hope.

Near the outskirts of town, the grass turned into mud, trampled by hundreds of horses, wagons, and buggies. New Hope was only a fraction of the size of St. Louis, but it was a Western railroad terminus and a growing, thriving city. It would be possible, perhaps, for the Indian to lose himself in such a city.

O'Fallon also knew, however, that in many ways even the largest cities were small communities where it was difficult to keep a secret. Strangers of a certain type would always be suspicious.

Unfortunately, O'Fallon at this point would also fit into this category.

The city was in sight when he pulled off the road. O'Fallon glanced down at himself, and knew that any self-respecting lawman would throw him in jail for vagrancy, or worse, on appearance alone. The rain had washed some of the mud from his clothes, but they were torn and dirty. He was still bloody in places, and he hadn't shaved in days. It would be difficult to slip into town unobserved, much less start asking questions about the Indian.

He rode slowly into town, which was strangely quiet because of the rain. The streets were nothing but mud, and only a few people were visible. This part of town consisted mainly of cheap houses of ill-repute and saloons. O'Fallon stopped at the first livery he came to and rode into the shelter. For the first time in days, he was in the dry, but barely. The roof leaked and the stalls had not been cleaned out for several days. Normally, O'Fallon would not have looked twice at such an establishment, but now he had little choice. An older man emerged from the darkness and squinted at him.

"Two bits," he said in a quarrelsome tone. "Two bits in advance, and extra for the hay. If you can't handle that, take your business elsewhere."

O'Fallon was thankful that the old man was nearsighted, and couldn't see the shape he was in. On the other hand, the old man probably wouldn't have cared in any case, judging by the condition of the stables. O'Fallon pulled out some coins and handed them over.

"It's a fair price," O'Fallon lied. "Here's my payment in advance."

The old man took the coins, peered at them closely, and then suddenly became more agreeable.

"For this, I'll throw in a bucket of oats," he said. "Looks like you were caught in this damned rain."

"Yeah, a little," O'Fallon admitted. "I need a place to stay and get cleaned up. You have any suggestions?"

"Whatcha looking for? A woman? A bath? A soft bed? We've got them all in this town."

"First, I need a place to get cleaned up," O'Fallon said. He thought a minute, then added, "I've got an appointment with a man named Braddock. Know him?"

The old man laughed.

"Who doesn't know him? Since he took over the bank, he's foreclosed on half the town and surrounding countryside." He spit. "Hell, he kicked my own sister out of her home, and she's a widow woman these past ten years." He squinted at O'Fallon. "You ain't a friend of his, are you?"

"Fortunately not. I just have some business to transact with him."

"Good luck to you. That man's a snake if I've ever seen one. At this time of day, you can probably find him in his office at the bank."

The old man gave instructions to one of the more respectable hotels and the bank and moved back into the shadows. O'Fallon thanked him and found himself a clean pile of hay in a corner. He sat down, stretched his legs, and started to clean the mud from his gun in preparation for his visit with the banker, Braddock.

Chapter 12

Lancer stepped from the rain into Braddock's quiet office. The banker looked up from his papers, surprised, as the Indian closed the door behind him.

"What the hell are you doing here?" he said. "I thought you were smart enough to keep our business relationship circumspect."

"Yeah. You'd like that, wouldn't you."

Braddock frowned.

"I'm a busy man. Get to the point."

Lancer shook his head. His long black hair sent a shower of water to the floor.

"I'm here to give you a progress report. The plan is working perfectly. Quincy by now is at the house, ready for questioning."

"Good work. You were faster than I expected. My . . . stenographer was not to leave town until tomorrow morning, but that can be easily resolved. Your men understand that the questioning is not to start until my man arrives?"

Lancer waved his hand indifferently, and plopped down in one of the leather chairs. He stretched out one leg and draped it over the chair arm. Water dripped, darkening the leather.

"Something else you might want to know. Your friend that killed Hansen is still in the area. You don't have to worry about him, however. We scared him away." Lancer laughed. "Hell, if he can still walk, or run, he's probably taken off like a scalded dog away from here. We took care of him good."

"You didn't kill him?"

"Dunno. We left him unconscious in the mud. He may be dead. Anyways, he won't be bothering you again."

Braddock tapped his fingers impatiently on his desk. He said, "Why did you fool with him? Did he try to interfere with your work?"

"Naw. He was following Quincy, and doing an all-right job of it." He laughed, leaning back in the chair. "I just wanted to show him who was the best."

Braddock frowned again. He had a prickly feeling at the back of his neck, like he always had when a deal was going sour. He picked up a silver paperweight shaped like a coiled snake. The room was quiet as the rain started to let up outside.

"Very well. The information is noted. You still should never meet me in public, like this."

Lancer smiled, and flicked an imaginary speck of dust off his wet shirt.

"Yeah. Only I'm not so sure you're calling all the shots. Now that we're officially business partners, I think we need to—how would you say it?—renegotiate the terms."

Braddock returned the paperweight to the corner of his desk. He said, "I think you need to express yourself more clearly."

"You ain't been paying me shit to provide you with information. That was just small stuff. Now that I'm in a big time with you, I think it's time we upped the payments. I'm not some dumb ass like Hansen. I've already proven that by leaving O'Fallon in the mud. I think I deserve a bigger share in the game you're running."

"I don't think you know what you're asking," Braddock said.

"The hell I don't. I'm tired of playing your game. Now it's time I got some for myself."

Braddock leaned back in his chair, and opened his desk

drawer a few inches. The revolver was now within easy reach. He leaned beneath his desk, and loosened the boot knife.

"Very well," he said, leaning forward on his desk. "Let's talk."

O'Fallon took only a few minutes to clean his gun and insert fresh cartridges. Outside, the rain had almost stopped. He knew that the way he looked he could not simply walk through the best part of town and into the banker's private office. It was possible that he could be picked up for vagrancy.

O'Fallon knew he had only a few minutes to make his next move.

As a boy in Tennessee, Sean had never visited a real town, much less one the size of New Hope, which had boomed since the war. But O'Fallon was a fast learner. He had learned to hunt and track, but also to observe carefully, taking in minute details at a glance and to remember what he had seen. He had learned how to learn quickly. These skills, combined with an innate intelligence and curiosity, had once enabled O'Fallon to quickly become an accomplished soldier, tackling tricky and dangerous assignments.

His unit had been involved in a series of skirmishes in Missouri that required him and his fellow soldiers to occupy several small and larger towns. O'Fallon took the opportunity to learn as much as he could about the layout of towns, the townspeople, and the world outside the Tennessee mountains. The people were generally friendly enough, since most did not have strong political feelings. They just wanted to be left alone. If treated politely they would respond in kind, and O'Fallon's mother had always stressed manners along with the reading and writing.

The end result was that O'Fallon could be as comfortable in the city as the wilderness.

O'Fallon moved out from the livery, following back alleys as long as possible. The alleys seemed almost familiar to O'Fallon, since they were similar to dozens of others he had patrolled during the war.

A COLD, DARK TRAIL

The sun came out, and, sure enough, people started pouring into the street. Even in the back alleys he crossed paths with several people, who looked at him strangely.

The crowd noises got louder as O'Fallon neared the center of town. He spotted a rain barrel at the corner of one of the buildings. He stepped onto it with his good leg, reached up to the low-hanging roof. He tested his other leg. It hurt, but held him. He pulled himself up the slight slope, stepping lightly. The height gave him a perspective on the whole town. He easily spotted the bank building and reached it in minutes.

O'Fallon positioned himself near the edge, behind the wooden facade, and observed the scene below. The streets were still wet, and horses were kicking up mud on the wooden sidewalks. Most of the people, however, were going about their business, enjoying the sunshine. Nobody was aware of his presence. Voices could be heard faintly through the roof from inside the building below, but the words were muffled.

When the streets temporarily cleared and the alley beside the bank was deserted, O'Fallon gently dropped to the dirt. He landed on bent knees. He felt a slight twinge, but ignored it and quietly walked through the back door of the bank. The teller—bald, with wire-rimmed glasses—was bent over a drawer in his little cage, behind polished and carved wooden arches.

O'Fallon had little experience with bankers, but still did not particularly like them or their banks. This one was no exception. It smelled faintly of greenbacks and dust and resembled a tomb. It was dark; the only light filtered through barred windows onto polished wooden floors. O'Fallon glanced around, noted the door marked simply PRIVATE, and stepped toward it. The footsteps seemed to echo from the dark brown walls, but the teller didn't even glance at the visitor. O'Fallon firmly grasped the doorknob, turned it. As he expected, the door was not locked and opened smoothly on well-oiled hinges.

The Indian's back was to the door. Braddock was leaning forward across his desk, watching Lancer's face. Braddock looked up, surprised, as O'Fallon stepped into the room. Lancer continued talking.

". . . I'm worth the money to you," Lancer said. "Not many know the area as well as me."

O'Fallon walked across the floor, his footsteps silent on the carpet.

"You think not?" Braddock asked.

"I know—"

O'Fallon grabbed Lancer's shirt, pulled him from the chair, and spun him around. Lancer's mouth flew open and he said, "What are *you* doing—"

O'Fallon's fist lashed out and solidly hit Lancer's mouth. He fell backward across Braddock's desk, knocking papers and pens to the floor. Sean paid no attention to the desk, but pulled Lancer again to his feet. This time Lancer kicked out, but his foot missed, and O'Fallon threw him against the wall. He slumped to the floor, a trickle of blood running down his cheek.

Without another glance at the Indian, the Tennessee man crossed the floor with quick strides and put a cocked revolver to the banker's head. O'Fallon said, "Make a wrong move, and you're dead. Do you understand me?"

Braddock barely nodded. O'Fallon backed away to get a better look at the man. His face was pudgy and bland. He was big, and looked bulky, but O'Fallon guessed he had hidden strength: muscle disguised by fat and the expensive gray business suit. He remained calm, in spite of the gun O'Fallon aimed at him. The office, like the bank, seemed still and deathly quiet.

Braddock looked steadily at the gun, and O'Fallon sensed no fear or surprise. And then, suddenly, it seemed the banker became another person. He started to sweat, his hands started to tremble, his small eyes widened in surprise.

"I suppose you thought I'd be dead by now. Your hired thug, there, had his fun and left me in the mud. Your men just keep failing. What will your boss, Culver, think?"

"I don't know what you're talking about. I—"

A COLD, DARK TRAIL

O'Fallon lifted the Remington, pointed it again at the banker's head.

"Okay . . . okay. Just calm down. What do you want from me? Money? I will give you all we have, but most of it has been—"

Braddock was sweating profusely, even though the room was cool. A light knock sounded at the door and the banker almost jumped out of his chair. O'Fallon motioned with the gun, but said nothing.

"Mr. Braddock? Is anything wrong?"

It was the teller.

O'Fallon's eyebrow lifted in warning. The banker answered, "No, nothing is wrong. But I'm in the middle of a meeting. Just go on home. I'll close for the day." And then, in a firmer voice, "This time lock the door."

They could hear faint footsteps, then the sound of a door being closed and locked.

"Good job, Braddock. Now, how about some answers? I want information. I want to know where your men have taken Quincy. And I want you to tell me everything you know about your boss, Winston Culver."

The banker's voice trembled as he answered.

"I never said to kill you. I have no interest in you. I don't even know who you are. . . ."

O'Fallon sat on the corner of the desk, his eyes focused on Braddock. He said, "You know that Hansen failed his assignment, or you wouldn't have sent more men after him. And if you know that, you also know that I was the one who killed Hansen. That doesn't concern you? And you just saw me beat one of your men in your own office."

"I don't know anybody named Hansen. . . ."

"What about Quincy?"

Braddock nervously fiddled with the papers on his desk. He said, "I am a banker, a businessman, and Quincy just returned from a survey. I wanted to chat with him, and I was afraid you were holding him prisoner. . . ."

"You're a goddamned liar."

"He had information I wanted. That's all."

"Where did your men take him?"

"I don't know—"

O'Fallon slapped the banker's face with the back of his hand. The banker winced. His eyes shifted slightly as he thought.

"Why do you want to know?" The voice was a whimper.

"I heard your men talking." He gestured at Lancer, who was starting to moan and move slightly against the wall. "I know you plan to kill Quincy. I don't intend to let that happen. Now, you can tell me, and I'll let you live. Or I can shoot you and find him on my own."

O'Fallon placed the barrel of his gun against the pudgy cheek. He cocked the hammer and said, "I'm not going to ask a third time. Where is Quincy?"

"Don't kill me! Please don't kill me! He's at a house several miles north of here. It's the old Jarvis place."

"Now tell me about Culver."

The banker looked like he wanted to cry.

"I don't know anybody named Culver!" he wailed. "I've never even heard the name!"

O'Fallon pulled Braddock out of the plush chair and dragged him across the desk, scattering papers, pens, and a small silver paperweight shaped like a coiled snake. The object bounced off Sean's knee and boot before hitting the floor and rolling out of sight, but it was enough. It confirmed Braddock's connection to Culver.

O'Fallon finished dragging Braddock over the desk and then threw the man across the room. He landed with a crash against the far wall. He rubbed his neck, and then his legs, and said, "I tell you, I don't know anything! I'm just a banker! I don't know . . . Please don't kill me!"

O'Fallon paid no attention to Braddock's words, but in a sudden insane fury was standing over him. He kicked out with the toe of his boot, hitting the banker in the chin. His head snapped back. O'Fallon pulled the banker from the floor by his shirt collar and pounded his fist into the chubby face.

O'Fallon realized vaguely what he was doing, but didn't

care. Braddock was one of Culver's men, and he would have to die. O'Fallon again cocked the gun, placed it just inches from Braddock's head, but did not pull the trigger. Instead, he shook his head to clear it, and wondered what kind of man he was turning into.

Maybe, years before when the shock of his wife's death was new, he might have killed the banker in cold blood. Now, however, he paused. Braddock's face was puffy. His sobbing filled the room. O'Fallon wanted his revenge, but not at the expense of becoming a monster. He did not want to become the same type of man as Culver, Hansen, and Braddock.

O'Fallon had wasted enough time. By now, Quincy might be dead. And for what? So that Sean could get another *possible* clue to Culver.

O'Fallon uncocked the gun, and turned. He knew that by leaving at this time he would have to start the search for Culver all over again. Chances were, Braddock would be on the first train out of town as soon as O'Fallon left. But what choice did he have?

His foot kicked the pile of papers and the silver paperweight. He ground the object into the floor and said, "Next time there'll be no mercy. I'll kill you." He hit Braddock in the back of the head, knocking him unconscious, and stepped over the banker and the Indian toward the door.

Braddock was not unconscious. He was hurt, but had only pretended to be knocked out. He waited for several minutes, to be certain that O'Fallon had left. Only then did he roll over, groaning softly. He touched his head tenderly, and thought, The things I do for Culver!

This O'Fallon was dangerous. Braddock had no idea how he could have slipped through town and into his office without being seen or stopped. And he wondered how O'Fallon— a complete stranger on the scene—could have uncovered the banker's connection to the Culver organization.

Braddock sat up, no longer sweating and no longer acting afraid. Not that he had been afraid to start with. His chameleonlike abilities were just one of the values he brought to the Culver organization. It gained him some time, and by his reckoning allowed him to reveal nothing of importance. He did admit where Quincy was being held, but Quincy was no longer one of Braddock's concerns. O'Fallon had changed everything.

The situation was becoming more complicated. He had been mistaken about Lancer; the Indian had a loose mouth, and was not nearly as competent as he had thought. Even worse, Lancer was greedy. If left alone, he could be troublesome. Lancer had now opened his eyes and was starting to stand. Braddock, however, was not about to make the same mistake that Culver had made with Jack Hansen. Braddock pulled the gun from the drawer and shot the Indian once, between the eyes. A spray of gray and red exploded against the wall.

The sound was loud in the room, but Braddock knew that the shot would probably not be heard through the thick bank walls.

With that problem resolved, he considered the men holding Quincy. Braddock had not yet sent anybody to the Jarvis place, so there would be nothing there to tie him to the kidnapping. The men only knew that Lancer had hired them and that they were supposed to question the surveyor. Lancer had apparently carelessly used Braddock's name, but the word of some Indian thugs would not hold up as any kind of evidence in a white court.

For a long minute, Braddock had thought O'Fallon would pull the trigger. Anyone who could burn another man alive and then brag about it would not be concerned about blowing out a banker's brains. During those moments of uncertainty, Braddock's hand had sneaked toward his hidden boot knife. But then O'Fallon apparently had a change of heart, and Braddock decided to play possum. That O'Fallon had not tried to kill him was a puzzle, but one Braddock was not going to worry about.

The banker stood, smoothed his clothes, and walked to his desk, picking up some of the papers and utensils that had fallen to the floor. He fingered the smashed rattlesnake paperweight. Culver had placed Braddock in charge of the Indian Territory project. It had been a relatively straightforward job, especially considering his background in the government's Indian-affairs programs. Should he now try to cut his losses? Or just kill O'Fallon and continue as originally planned?

When Braddock first learned of Hansen's disappearance, and then of his death, he figured O'Fallon had gotten a lucky break. It was the only way a hillbilly from Tennessee could best a professional—even one as careless as Hansen.

But now?

O'Fallon no doubt represented a much larger group. His concern for Quincy made it seem obvious that he was, in fact, working for the Simpson organization. That meant a serious threat to Culver's new business enterprises. If O'Fallon was part of an operation, killing him would not solve any problems, since Simpson—or whomever O'Fallon worked for—would just send out more hired guns. O'Fallon had also bragged that Culver's organization would be destroyed. These were serious developments that the boss should know about. Culver would have more resources to determine who was behind O'Fallon, and the proper strategy to respond to the threat.

Braddock decided he should relay the information in person.

He figured the men holding Quincy would soon be dead, if they were not already. There was no use wasting any more valuable time on them, or attempting to get Quincy's information. The Indian Territory project would just have to continue from the Washington, D.C., end.

The final question was what to do about Lancer. Braddock decided to try and place the blame on O'Fallon. By making a formal complaint, and directing the federal marshal to the old Jarvis place to pick up O'Fallon and Quincy, a night in jail for O'Fallon was almost guaranteed. That would allow Braddock time to catch the evening train to St. Louis and be the first to break the news to Culver.

Chapter 13

The sun was bright as O'Fallon arrived at the Jarvis place. Now that the sun had finally returned, the air had warmed and the ground had started to dry, even though the smell of wet leaves remained in the air. Sean had slipped past the crowds back to the livery, where the old man was more than happy to give him exact directions.

"Yeah, that was a decent family," the old man said. "But Braddock wanted the land, and kicked them out. He's a heartless son of a bitch, I tell you that. He'd have this old place, too, if it was worth having."

Sean had retrieved his horse and gear and left before the stableman could ask him how the business had gone with the banker. O'Fallon, unfortunately, had to leave his packs and packhorse behind, so that he could make better time. His main concern now, however, was to rescue Quincy and to get on with his hunt for Culver.

O'Fallon hoped he wasn't too late. Now, he thought that maybe he should have trailed Quincy instead of the Indian. Maybe a few years ago he would have had no doubts. Quincy was nothing to him, and had been nothing except a potential lead to Culver. He had abandoned Quincy to follow a more likely path. Would the little information he had found, however, be worth Quincy's life?

The horse raced across the land. O'Fallon automatically watched for gullies from the recent rain, but his mind was

A COLD, DARK TRAIL

also reviewing what he had discovered. He was positive that Braddock knew more than he had said; the telltale sign was the small rattlesnake paperweight. It was surely not just a coincidence that the banker had on his desk the symbol used by Culver during his renegade days. Slowly but surely O'Fallon had been working his way up through Culver's organization: from Hansen, to Braddock, and then hopefully to Culver. But now he had probably lost the trail by trying to rescue Quincy from Braddock's men.

Sean had not yet figured how to take that next step. It was one thing to trail hired thugs like Hansen and Lancer through the wilds; it was something else to follow the subtle trails of deceit left by "civilized" men like Braddock. Braddock, and Culver, would also have other resources to insulate them from the rest of the world. How else could Culver have remained out of sight for so long after the war? O'Fallon had few resources he could call on, but he would find a way. He hadn't come this far to fail now.

He halted his horse about a half mile from the farmhouse and walked the rest of the way. He figured guards would be posted near the house itself, and he wanted to get a feel of the surrounding area.

The Jarvis place had the makings of a productive farm. Unlike the hills where O'Fallon had lived as a boy, this country was relatively flat, with a good mixture of pasture, woods, and tillable land. A few fences had been built, but the fields and pastures were vacant. The Jarvis family had apparently been hard workers and could have made a real success of this place, except for Braddock foreclosing early on the mortgage. From a business standpoint, it made little sense, but O'Fallon knew that Braddock's plans for this farm had nothing to do with agriculture and everything to do with his unsavory business.

The house itself was relatively luxurious: solid frame construction, glass windows. Now, it also showed faint signs of neglect. Mud on the porch had not been swept off. A bucket had been carelessly tossed to one side of the house. The paint was faded. A few of the windows were cracked. From Braddock's standpoint, the location of the house would be another plus. It was situated in a large clearing on a rise, so that any approaching visitors could be easily seen, unless, like O'Fallon, they came in through the woods. A large barn was located several hundred feet behind the house, but the only livestock in it were the horses of Quincy's captors.

O'Fallon climbed a large oak tree near the edge of the woods to gain a clearer picture of the situation. In his youth, O'Fallon had learned patience. He could remain motionless for hours, waiting for a squirrel or deer to show itself. That skill was more difficult now because of the dull throb in his leg, but still served him well as he observed the farmhouse.

It was only lightly guarded. One man was stationed in the barn loft. It was a good spot, giving him a view of most of the clearing and of the house itself, allowing him opportunity to pick off any intruders. Still, O'Fallon was surprised that there was only one guard; they must have been feeling very confident.

An hour passed, and O'Fallon determined that only two more were in the house. Each came out periodically to relieve himself and to wave a signal to the man in the barn. Soon, O'Fallon observed a flurry of movement in one of the side rooms: the figures paced back and forth in front of the window, at times even pausing long enough to give O'Fallon a clean shot, had he wanted to solve the problem in that way. He wasn't prepared to take action yet. He wanted to avoid more killing, if he could. He had been tempted to kill Braddock, but had stopped himself in time. O'Fallon had never killed a man in cold blood. He had never liked killing, and never would, with the exception of Winston Culver. He would kill these men if he had to, but he preferred to let them live.

The afternoon sun was bright, and cast dark shadows on the ground. He wanted to make his move quickly, but he knew that he had to wait until the sun started to set.

As the shadows finally stretched across the ground and the night birds began to call, O'Fallon shimmied down the oak and started toward the barn. He moved easily from shadow to shadow, with barely a sound, from the oak, to a clump of elderberries, to a thick stand of weeds that had been allowed to grow near the barn.

O'Fallon paused, watching the barn loft. The guard shifted and was still again. The shadows were longer, darker.

O'Fallon moved toward an open side door of the barn and stepped inside, barely breathing.

The smell of hay and of fresh manure greeted him. Apparently when the Jarvis family were forced from their home they had left a full barn in anticipation of winter. Hay was stacked almost to the ceiling and feed bins were full of grain.

Above him, the sentry shifted slightly, sending down a scattering of hay. In the stalls across the barn were the four horses, pacing impatiently in place, switching their tales as slow-moving flies, dulled by the autumn air, buzzed and landed on sleek hide.

O'Fallon waited patiently, planning his moves with care.

The loft was open. The hay that had been stored in the front had been used, providing space for the guard. O'Fallon could reach it from where he had crouched, but the noise would reveal his presence too soon. He wanted to surprise the guard, knock him out as quickly as possible, and then move on to the house. The ladder leading to the loft was still a half-dozen yards away, toward the front of the barn.

The horses paced again. A gruff voice called down, "Hey, easy down there, dammit. Easy." The horses pricked their ears, but otherwise ignored the orders. One horse tried to reach over the stall to nip another. The voice yelled again, "Calm down, unless you want the shit beat out of you."

O'Fallon decided to lure the guard closer to him. He edged toward the feed bins in the corner of the room where he was waiting. He reached in, pulled out a handful of grain, held it up to where the horses could see.

The pacing in place continued.

O'Fallon tossed the feed, and then several other handfuls, in quick succession to the horses over the stall walls. Quincy's horse, apparently more jitterish than the others, started to kick. Overhead, the guard grumbled and started to walk toward the ladder.

"Damned critters," he growled. "Why can't they control themselves—"

O'Fallon at once jumped on the feed barrel and, using it as a springboard, grabbed the floor of the loft. He pulled himself up and was on the guard as he turned, surprised. O'Fallon hit the other man in the stomach, doubling him over, and then threw a hard punch to the head, knocking out the guard. Sean tossed some hay to the horses, to calm them down, and then dragged the unconscious sentry toward the back.

The whole incident had taken less than sixty seconds. He moved to the edge of the barn and checked the house. It remained quiet. So far, so good.

O'Fallon quickly tied the man's hands with a rope hanging on the barn wall and then climbed down the ladder.

One of the most difficult parts of the attack was now over; the men in the house felt secure, and would have only a careless watch, if any. The growing darkness also helped to cover Sean's movement from the barn to the window of the room where he thought Quincy was being held prisoner. He crouched beneath the window, then changed to a kneeling position, to ease the pressure on his leg.

The house was quiet, so O'Fallon took a chance and looked inside.

The room had apparently been a parlor, with some nice furniture left behind. It was a matched set, sturdily built, with a flowery covering. Quincy was tied to a straight-backed kitchen chair in the middle of the room. After several minutes, Quincy's two captors entered and O'Fallon lowered his head to beneath the windowsill. The larger one slapped Quincy on the cheek. The sound made a loud pop.

"I'd like to start the questioning now," he said, chuckling. "I'm all ready to go. Waddya say, Oxman?"

O'Fallon heard another pop and more laughing.

"Dunno, Bridger," the other man said. "Lancer said to wait until somebody joined us from town. Supposed to write down the information, or something."

"Well, I'm tired of waiting. Who's the boss of this thing?"

"Dunno. All I care about is the money."

"Me? I'm looking for a little fun out of this. What do you think, Mr. Quincy?" No answer. "Oh, not talking? Not very friendly, is he?"

Suddenly O'Fallon heard a muffled blow, probably to the belly, followed by a groan.

"Hey, Bridger, leave off the rough stuff for a while."

"Just having a little fun."

O'Fallon raised his head to chance a quick look through the window. Quincy was red-faced, but remained calm. Quincy had gotten lucky, and the two men had not started their "questioning" in earnest. Bridger was a big man, and both he and Oxman wore guns. The room had only one entrance; O'Fallon could see the kitchen beyond the open door. So he would have to make his move through the rear of the house.

Sean crawled through the bushes at the side of the house, then stood and moved quickly. The back door was unlocked, but creaked slightly as it opened. It sounded explosively loud to O'Fallon, but apparently went unnoticed inside. He moved quickly and silently through the dark kitchen to where Quincy was being held. He could hear soft thuds as Bridger delivered more blows.

"Leave him alone for a while. . . ."

"Shut up and get out of my way! I'm in charge, now. . . ."

O'Fallon kicked open the door. The two captors turned, surprised. Bridger reached for his gun, but his movements were slow and clumsy. O'Fallon shot once, into Bridger's gun arm.

The other man's arms leaped into the air, his gun still in its holster.

It took several seconds for Quincy to recognize his rescuer. Sean's clothes were torn and covered with dried mud and blood. His hair was matted. His face was covered with a rough beard. Finally, he said, "I'm glad to see you again, even if you are a sight for sore eyes."

"It's been a long trip," O'Fallon said. "I'm glad I made

it in time." He gestured to the smaller Indian and said, "Remove your gun belt. And untie Quincy."

Oxman obeyed, but he answered, "Lancer won't like this. He warned you about interfering. He'll kill you."

"I don't much think so. I left him unconscious back in town, in Braddock's office."

All three of the other men looked shocked.

"You beat Lancer?" the smaller man said.

Bridger was holding his arm, trying to stop the bleeding, but still managed to laugh harshly. He said, "He's lying. If he ran into Lancer, the fool must have let him go." He paused, then, and in a softer voice said, "But why? And . . . what about McGill? How did he get past McGill, out in the barn . . ."

Quincy shook loose the ropes that had held him, retrieved the gun and gun belt from the floor.

"How'd you make it to New Hope and back out here so soon?" Quincy asked, rubbing his arms to return the circulation. "I'd say that would be close to impossible. And what's this about Braddock?"

O'Fallon quickly ran down the events that had taken place since they had left Parkersburg, including the fact that O'Fallon had been trailing Quincy.

"Yeah, I had the feeling I was being watched, but I could never find you," Quincy answered. "I thought it might be some of these yahoos, but couldn't figure why they were waiting so long to make their move. After a while, I figured I was imagining things. I let my guard down, and they got me without even a fight. They didn't hurt me too bad, though. Fortunately, you got here in time."

"I'm going out to get my horse, and bed him down for the night in the barn. I'll bring in the other fellow that I have tied up in the barn, and some more rope to take care of these two. Watch them, and don't hesitate to shoot."

"With pleasure."

O'Fallon headed back through the kitchen, when almost by instinct he jumped to one side of the window.

A bullet broke through the glass, whizzing past his head.

"Bring them in here, where we can watch them!" O'Fallon ordered. "We're being shot at."

Quincy followed the two Indians into the room, and directed them into the corner. O'Fallon brushed the shattered glass to one side and kneeled by the window. Finally, a voice called out from the barn, "All of you in the house! Come out with your hands above your heads!"

The voice was loud, sharp, clear, with authority.

O'Fallon said softly to Quincy, "Looks like your enemies found us again. Damned, how many are there? Are they all Culver's men, in one way or another? Maybe I should have shot Braddock and Lancer. . . ."

Quincy said, "I think you should know—"

"Just do as I say. Find something to tie up these two. Here—" He pulled down an old curtain and tossed it to Quincy, who did as he was told. O'Fallon then made a quick search of the house. There were too many windows, too much area to protect, and no cover for escape. He figured the enemy were all around the house; they had him trapped. But he wasn't about to lose, not with unfinished business still before him.

"Don't think you can shoot your way out," the voice yelled. "You can't. Don't even try it." When O'Fallon didn't respond, the voice continued, "We'll give you five minutes to come out."

"No."

Quincy said, "Shut up and listen to me, Sean. That man out there—"

"Do you hear that?" O'Fallon interrupted. "One of them is trying to sneak in on us. Listen."

O'Fallon creeped along the wall, toward the door. He sat on the floor, rested the gun on his knees, aimed at the door. His voice was now a whisper.

"He thinks he can sneak up on us, like I did to you all. But I'm paying a little closer attention. He'll be in for a surprise. These guys beat me once, and kidnapped you. I don't intend to let that happen again." He paused, and listened. "Ssh. He's about to make his move!"

As if on cue, the door burst open. O'Fallon shot once, but his aim was off: Quincy's hand had reached out, knocked the gun to one side. The man in the door now had the advantage. His gun was aimed at O'Fallon's heart.

"Don't move, mister. For your own good, don't move."

O'Fallon raised his hands, looked at Quincy with fire in his eyes, but said nothing, even after he spotted the bright silver badge on the chest of the man in the doorway.

Chapter 14

The marshal and a deputy led the way. Behind them rode O'Fallon and Quincy. Their hands were free, but their guns had been removed. Bridger and his companions followed in handcuffs. Another deputy was at the rear of the group. Stars shining overhead showed the road back to town.

Little had been said since leaving the farm.

"Why are you arresting us?" O'Fallon had demanded.

The marshal was a man named Bill Ernst. He was tall, muscular, with a large mustache. He said, "You're being held on suspicion. There's a dead Indian in Braddock's office, and Braddock claimed you did the shooting."

"That's a lie. When I was there, I—"

"Hold on a minute, son. I'm bringing you in for investigation, to sort out this mess. I'd advise you to not say anything that might hurt you."

O'Fallon was glad that Quincy had prevented him from shooting a law officer. He was not pleased, however, at losing Culver's trail again. He had succeeded in saving Quincy, but at what cost? He wouldn't be able to pick up the trail again from a jail cell. O'Fallon had no illusions. He was a stranger in town and had become the enemy of one of the more influential men there. He had nobody to come to his aid and no money to buy a legal defense.

Quincy rode along peacefully, smoking his cigar.

"In all my life, I've never been behind bars," O'Fallon

finally said. His voice was low. "You're mighty relaxed about this whole thing. Remember, I may be the one charged, but you're in the middle of all this."

"I know. But I'm not worried. And neither should you be." Quincy puffed on his cigar. "What you want now is to find Culver, right? Well, what would you say if I told you that you're now closer to finding Culver than ever before? And that I could provide you a crystal-clear, direct path, right to his door. Would you be interested?"

"What the hell are you talking about?"

"Sean O'Fallon, you're one of the most intelligent and most talented men I have ever run across. I do believe that you could have gotten us out of that trap that the marshal set up for us. But killing Bill would definitely be a bad move." Quincy puffed some more, then continued, "What you don't realize is that a lot more is going on here than just your search for vengeance. Most people have no idea what the real situation is. I think, though, that you can understand what I'm about to tell you."

"Go on."

"Most of it you know. About how many want the Indian lands opened up. It's only a matter of time before they are, you know. Who do you think will finally own the land? The farmers? The cattlemen? No, they think too small. The future is in the hands of the men who think big, and can act."

"Men like you?"

"Hell, no. I'm only an engineer from Boston. I don't have the temperament to be a tycoon or a land baron. A lot of Byzantine politics is taking place. Indian leaders are divided, Washington politicians are being bought and sold, new faces pop up and old faces disappear. Alliances and power bases are shifting almost daily." Quincy lowered his voice even more. "My boss, Henry Simpson, is one of the current powers. And who do you think got Bill his position? Simpson. Ernst is an ally. Hell, he's practically on the payroll."

The voices had been low. Quincy raised his voice slightly and said, "Bill?"

"What's up, Quince?"

"Come over here for a few minutes, would you? You might be interested in O'Fallon's story."

Ernst moved his horse closer. A deputy dropped back to keep a sharper watch on the other prisoners. O'Fallon hesitated at first, so Quincy urged, "Go ahead and tell Bill what you told me. You saved my life—twice. I'm not going to steer you wrong now."

O'Fallon shrugged, and quickly told of his search for Culver, how the trail led to his fight with Lancer, Braddock, and the two fellow Cherokee prisoners. Ernst listened with interest.

"I know about Culver," he said. "I've received information similar to yours, that he's active in the territory, or trying to be. But you thought he was rampaging like the old days. He's a little more slick than that, these days. Now he's trying to steal the land legally. Braddock is a former Indian agent that's looking out for Culver's interests in this part of the country. He's active through agents, accomplices, underlings. He's the one that sent the men after Quincy."

"It doesn't make sense," O'Fallon said. "Culver's nothing but a common criminal."

"Don't forget that many 'great' men started out as criminals," Quincy added.

"Culver apparently took his spoils from the war and invested them wisely," Ernst continued. "I understand he's doing quite well for himself, growing in wealth and power. He's opened a business in St. Louis, and is constructing a new building to prove his respectability. He's cultivating the rich and powerful; rumor has it that he may be looking to the Senate, or beyond. He's making all the right moves."

O'Fallon scowled.

"You seem to know an awful lot about Culver. Where were you when they were beating up Quincy?"

"We've known about Braddock's connection to Culver for a long time, but we didn't expect the physical attacks on Quincy. If we had known it was coming to this, we would have taken steps."

The dark outline of the town came into view, which cut

off any further conversation. Quincy and Ernst moved slightly ahead, and talked in whispers. As they approached the jail, Ernst said, "You'll spend the rest of the night in jail. I can't ignore a complaint made by one of the town's leading citizens. But with luck I'll have my investigation wrapped up by morning."

The jail was relatively new, but already smelled of urine and vomit. The marshal had placed O'Fallon and Quincy in one cell and the other prisoners in the third cell. The middle cell was left empty.

The rays of the early morning sun edged through the outside window. O'Fallon sat with his back to the cool wall, thinking about what Ernst and Quincy had told him on the ride back to town. He had somehow gotten lucky. Instead of losing the trail to Culver, he now possibly had a direct lead to him. Ernst, or some other of Simpson's men, would be able to tell him exactly where Culver was located. Or O'Fallon could find him on his own. Ernst said Culver was putting up a new office building, which could easily be found. It was almost too good to be true.

O'Fallon was excited. He was also still in jail. That worried him.

Outside the cell, the town started to wake. From down the street came sounds of water being drawn from wells and of breakfast pots and pans. Quincy yawned, stretched, and opened his eyes. He reached into his pocket, pulled and lit a cigar. He placed one foot on the floor and said, "You still awake? You shouldn't worry so much." Movement came from the other cell, but Quincy and O'Fallon ignored it. "I've been thinking about your situation. I owe you—double. To show my appreciation for your help, I'll recommend you to my superiors. Ernst sent the telegram this morning. I expect an answer before too long. You joining up with Simpson could help everybody." O'Fallon remained impassive, so Quincy tried a different approach. He asked, "What do you think about Maria?"

"I think she's a very special woman. What's it to you?"

"I got to know her, Parker, and a lot of the others during my stay on the nation's lands. Before I left she spoke very highly of you. If you join our organization, we'll help you find Culver, and find some assignments for you in the nation. We might even find a place for you and Maria to—"

O'Fallon was off his cot and had Quincy's shirt collar before the other man could even take the cigar from his mouth.

"You leave her out of this," O'Fallon said. His voice was quiet, which made his words even more threatening. "I don't want her hurt."

"Neither do I, Sean," Quincy said, his voice also quiet. "She'll do what she thinks is right. You know that."

O'Fallon loosened his grip on Quincy's shirt.

"Yeah. Sorry."

The talk was interrupted by a rattle of keys, as Ernst swung the door open.

"You're both free to go," he said.

"Hey! What about us? We're innocent—" Bridger yelled from the other cell.

"Shut your damned mouth unless you're spoken to," Ernst said. Then, to O'Fallon, he continued, "Braddock left town without filing formal charges against you. In any case, it looks like you killed the Indian in self-defense."

"But I didn't kill the man," O'Fallon protested. "When I left, he was unconscious . . ."

"Whatever," Ernst said, then handed an envelope to Quincy as he stepped from the cell. "Here's your telegram, Quince."

"Thanks."

The two walked into the morning air. It was cool, with the smell of sawdust, wood smoke, and approaching winter. Quincy opened the envelope, read the telegram, and said to O'Fallon, "You're in."

"No."

"I mean, you're on the payroll."

"I said, 'No.' "

Quincy scratched his thinning hair before pulling on his

hat. "Don't you understand? We're offering you a direct route to Culver!"

"Maybe I'll help you, and maybe I won't. But I don't want to work for you or Simpson or anybody. What I'm doing, I'm doing for my own reasons. I'll not be controlled by any man, for any amount of money, for any reason."

Quincy scratched his head again.

"Do you realize you're turning down an offer made to very few men?"

"Makes no difference. I'll fight my own battles."

"Then you can tell Mr. Simpson that in person." Quincy pulled out his watch. "Simpson moves fast. His train should arrive here about noon." Quincy chuckled. "One of the advantages of owning your own railroad. Do you really want to turn down those kinds of resources?"

"I'll talk with him tonight," O'Fallon said, finally.

"That's good! And in the meantime?"

"I'm going to check on my horses, and my gear. Then I am going to eat breakfast, get cleaned up, and get some new clothes. And a pipe."

"And you'll think about the offer?"

"I'm willing to meet Simpson. Doesn't hurt anything to talk."

Bridger was standing on the cot and had stretched to his full height to watch O'Fallon and Quincy walk down the street.

"I'll show those bastards," Bridger said. He stepped to the floor. "He may have beat Lancer, but he won't beat me."

Oxman said, "Yeah? We're lucky he didn't kill us."

The third prisoner said, "I say forget about him. You shut up fast enough when he put that bullet in you. You're lucky that wound ain't serious."

Bridger lifted his arm, moved it over his head. He said, "It ain't nothing. What's important is what that bastard is doing." The others looked at him blankly. Bridger glared, and continued, "Didn't you hear what they were saying? That bastard didn't just get it over us, or Braddock, they're also farting at Culver. He's a bigwig back in St. Louis trying to get his claws into the nation. That got me to thinking, and I have a plan." He stepped down from the cot. "Don't you think Braddock and Culver would love to see that bastard brought to his knees? So far, Jack Hansen couldn't do it, and Lancer couldn't do it. But we can do it."

"Why try?"

"Lancer used to talk about how we had to be on the right side when the territory was taken over by the whites. It makes sense to me. Seems like Culver may be the man. We kill O'Fallon, we impress the right people, we have our in."

"We surprised O'Fallon once, in the rain, but I doubt we can ever do that again," Oxman said. "He snuck up on us damned good at the farmhouse. He got McGill in the barn without even working up a sweat. It'll take more than a simple bushwhacking with O'Fallon."

"Every man has a weak spot. With O'Fallon it's a woman. And you know who they were talking about, don't you? Maria Rushing, that damned woman with her nose always in the air, like she's too good for the rest of us. She made a fool of me once, and I swore I'd get even with her. Maybe I can have some fun and get O'Fallon, to boot."

"What makes you think O'Fallon gives a damn?"

"Didn't you see the way he acted when she was mentioned? We can get to him through her. If we can deliver her to Braddock's and Culver's front door, then Mr. Sean O'Fallon would come following right behind. He would have to save her, wouldn't he? So when he plays hero, we'll just make sure that this time he won't walk away."

"You really think it'll work?"

"Of course it'll work. What could go wrong?"

Oxman shrugged.

"What about you, McGill?"

"Count me out."

Bridger scowled, stood back on the cot, and looked out the window. He said, "Suit yourself. The two of us can do it. We'll crush the bastard right in front of Braddock and

Culver. That way they'll be sure to let us join their group, and when they take control of the nation, we'll be sitting pretty."

Chapter 15

Winston Culver looked out over the crowd. He felt a sense of power greater even than when he had led his Raiders to victory after victory during the war. The most important people within a five-hundred-mile radius of St. Louis were at the party—some from as far east as Chicago. It would be the talk of St. Louis society for months to come.

His plan was working! He had progressed from Civil War hero to established businessman and now to political leader. His agents were everywhere, keeping him informed by wire and rail of the latest developments, working for his interests, serving him. True, some of the newspapers painted his war exploits in rather lurid terms, but for the first few years after the war he had kept a low profile. He had placed his men and developed his plans, as the emotions of the war started to die down to a manageable level. But now, with this party, he was announcing to all the world that Winston Culver was once again in action! He was only thirty-three years old, and if his plan continued to succeed, he would be in the White House within twenty years.

Not bad for a bastard from Charleston.

His plans for the Indian Territory were just a part of his overall dreams, just another tool to gain him the power, prestige, and respectability he craved. The Indian Territory project was a long-range plan; his more immediate concern was to complete the new office building on the banks of the Mississippi, and to further his respectability in the eyes of the business and political leaders of St. Louis and the state.

Judging from the sparkling jewels and expensive clothes before him, Culver decided he did not have to worry. They were already in the palm of his hand. The party, including the chamber orchestra providing the music, cost a fortune. It was worth every penny.

Culver stepped into the swirling sea of people, to mingle. He lifted two glasses of wine from the tray of the passing butler, turned to the woman standing next to him.

"Mrs. Richards?" he said.

She looked up, as he handed one of the glasses to her.

"Why, thank you, Winston!"

Mrs. Richards was an older woman, overweight, with a round face and frown lines. She was also the wife of a prominent district judge, and so deserved attention. He knew that Judge Richards had a young mistress, but Culver also knew that even in these cases, wives could still wield great influence over their husbands. Sometimes, the presence of a mistress in the background could provide a wife even more influence than normal.

"We've all been watching your new building being constructed," she said. "It will be a most welcome addition to the city."

"Thank you. When it is completed, I promise to conduct an even bigger party. You and your husband, of course, will be among my honored guests. You will always be welcome in my offices, just as you are here in my home."

The woman sipped daintily. Rumor had it that she could put away a fifth of whiskey per day behind closed doors. His agents had confirmed the rumor: his dollars had loosened the tongues of a number of liquor suppliers.

"Why, sir, this wine is excellent! What vintage is it?"

"It is a '57, from my own vineyards," he answered.

Mrs. Richards giggled. The night was still young, but this was far from her first drink.

"Why, Winston, you surely jest! You also own property in France?"

Culver smiled and touched the woman lightly on the elbow. Mrs. Richards smiled back and fluttered her eyes. He said, "No, I own some property in the Missouri Valley, some miles from here."

"Impossible! This wine is almost as good as my husband's French imports!"

"The best wines are from France, just as the best women are from St. Louis," Culver said, bowing slightly. He thought, What shit! But his words had the desired effect. The woman giggled, and blushed, and moved a half step closer to Culver. He continued, "I recently purchased a number of acres along the Missouri River, about a hundred miles from here. The area is a German community, noted for their vintner's skills."

The woman giggled again and said, "Oh, Winston, you're so learned!"

He motioned to the butler, gave Mrs. Richards a new glass, and said, "Excuse me, but I see your husband. I must talk to him. I don't want him to think I'm after his beautiful wife!"

Mrs. Richards giggled again, and downed the contents of the glass.

Culver moved easily to the side of Judge Richards.

"Please excuse Beulah," Richards said. "I hope she's not bothered you terribly."

"Not at all, sir. We were talking about wine. She seemed to enjoy the vintage I am serving."

"She does enjoy her spirits." The judge sighed. "She often enjoys them too much. But I must admit, you do have good taste in wine."

"I am having my man deliver two cases of this vintage to you tomorrow, with your permission, of course. One will be to your home, for Mrs. Richards's enjoyment. And the second case will be delivered to your office, for use as you see fit."

The judge laughed.

"You are very astute, son. Very astute, and very discreet. I like that in a man."

"I'm willing to help you in any other way I can, as well.

Don't forget, I do have banking interests and would be happy to work with you on . . . low-interest loans. Feel free to call on me at any time."

The judge slapped Culver on the back, laughed, and then hailed somebody across the crowded room.

Culver smiled to himself, satisfied. It took so little, sometimes. A small favor could yield great returns.

A tall, gaunt gentleman called out, "Winston!"

"Congressman!"

Culver smiled and shook hands as he worked his way through the crowd to Congressman Raddle's side.

"Quite a party, Winston." The congressman sipped his drink: bourbon, straight. "I'd like to thank you for your campaign contribution. It was most generous."

"I believe in supporting those who, like me, share the vision of this country's great future. We must all stand together and develop the country for the good of all."

"True. Most people have such limited vision. They can't see the good of our plans, even when it's spelled out for them. They can't seem to understand that the Western lands, if opened, could provide homes and farms for a great many people."

"It is good to see that men like you represent us on the Hill."

Raddle took another drink.

"Opposition is still great on the Hill, and in the administration, I'm afraid. The Cherokee Nation has a much stronger lobby than we had anticipated. That they had allied themselves with the Confederates during the war has weakened their position, but they still have a number of excellent politicians. To see them and hear them talk, you'd think they were white men."

"They are opposed to opening up the territory?"

"Some of them. And some are just holding out for bigger pieces of the pie. Others in the administration are smelling profits, so are blocking us, in the hope that they can benefit, as well. The situation is very confusing, and changing almost daily. Don't expect quick results."

A COLD, DARK TRAIL 135

"I'm a patient man. It's gotten me to where I am today. I'm willing to work with you."

The congressman's gaunt face looked somber.

"You still don't quite understand the situation, Winston. The opposition involves more than just a few bureaucrats. There are major, behind-the-scenes powers, trying to position themselves."

"Men like Henry Simpson?"

"He has a great many friends in the capital. He is a very important factor."

"Would greater resources help?"

"It is the only thing that will help. Many are still undecided, and the proper resources, directed to the right people, could sway many votes and gain much influence in the administration."

Culver did not hesitate a second. He said, "Consider it done. I will have one of my top men start on it first thing tomorrow. And, incidentally, I am forwarding an additional contribution to your campaign."

"We will succeed, Winston. It will not be easy, but the West will be ours."

Raddle turned, and walked to another small group of people.

Culver was still smiling, but his mind was racing. He was not really worried; this was just one more problem to be worked out. He had not come this far to let a little thing like political opposition stop him. And as for Simpson, Culver was certain the businessman would play fairly, which would be a chink in his armor.

He placed his half-empty glass on the table and noticed a new, unexpected guest.

Braddock, his man in charge of the Indian Territory project, stood in front of the open glass parlor doors. He was not unwelcome, for Culver had already decided to call Braddock back, to oversee the new business in Washington, D.C. But what was he doing here already?

Braddock looked distinguished in his suit coat, vest, and tie. He carried his pounds well, and had a sophisticated air as he walked into the room. He greeted many on a first-name basis, for in this world he was known as an influential, behind-the-scenes political troubleshooter. The ability to serve a variety of roles, as needed, was one of his invaluable traits.

Finally, the two men were standing side by side, in front of the small flames in the fireplace.

Culver said, "I'm surprised to see you."

"We have a problem."

"Something that couldn't be handled by telegram?"

"Apparently you're not the only person interested in the territory. You have some competition. Somebody with a lot of influence." Braddock's voice got even lower, and was almost lost, even to Culver, in the din of the party. "I sense the hand of Henry Simpson."

"In my den. Ten minutes."

Culver continued to circulate before quietly exiting the party. He walked down the hall and through the carved doors leading to the den. It was cool and quiet compared to the crowded party in the other rooms. He turned up the new gas lights. They cast a warm glow on the dark wood walls. He sat on the black leather chair and looked out the window, toward the river, to where the symbol of the new Winston Culver was nearly completed.

In a few minutes, Braddock lightly tapped on the doors and, without waiting for an answer, stepped through. He closed the doors behind him.

"So what's the problem?" Culver said.

"I think Simpson caught on to your plans. One of his people stopped Hansen and a group of my men. Hell, he even connected me to you. Only Simpson would have the power to know so much, so quickly."

Culver clipped the end of a cigar, leaned back in his chair. Braddock accepted a cigar, lit the end of Culver's cigar, then his own.

"What do you mean, he stopped Hansen?"

"He beat the man to a bloody pulp, shot him, and then burned him before he even had a chance to stop breathing."

The only surprise Culver showed was a brief interruption of the puffs of smoke swirling around his head. He said, "Hell."

"Hansen was one of your original Raiders," Braddock said.

"He was a tough one, when he wasn't drinking or whoring. I find it hard to believe one man could have beat him."

"I don't know where Simpson found this fellow, but he tracked one of my men to my office and . . . killed one of my key people. I sent him on a wild-goose chase, and for all I know he may have killed more of my men. He kept us from getting that survey information we needed."

Culver blew smoke into the air.

"Do you know who this gunfighter is?"

"The name's Sean O'Fallon. Ever hear of him?"

"No."

The sounds of the party could be heard faintly through the wooden doors. Culver was silent as he considered the new information. Braddock waited quietly by the door, enjoying the cigar. Culver finally said, "There is no permanent damage done. Hansen was an asset, but can be replaced. We can work around the lack of information that Simpson's survey would have provided. But this is the second time in less than thirty minutes that I've been warned about Simpson. A few years ago, I would have simply had him killed. It's not that easy any more." The two men smoked quietly for several more minutes. Culver continued, "I need you here in St. Louis for a few weeks, and then in Washington, to make sure that the necessary resources get into the right hands to pass the bills we need. At the same time, see if you can find out what Simpson is up to. I'll have some of my agents do a little digging on their own. This O'Fallon character couldn't have materialized out of thin air."

Braddock said, "I never knew of Simpson to use hired guns."

"The stakes are high. We all use whatever weapons we have to achieve our ends."

"What about O'Fallon? Word has it he also has some kind of grudge against you, as well."

Culver stood, and stretched. His shadow was dark against the wall.

"I'm not going to worry about one hired gun. So what if he's killed a few men? Maybe he was tougher than Hansen, but Hansen may have been careless. Guns are cheap. Talk is cheap."

"In the meantime?"

"Join the party. Circulate, see what you can find out. By now, tongues should be pretty loose. We'll work out the details tomorrow."

Braddock placed the cigar back in his mouth and let himself out of the room.

Culver stood, walked to the window. The lights of the city twinkled, and in the distance he could see the black outline of his new building. Everything up to now had been going well. These new developments were disappointing, but they were not serious. He would, however, have to reconsider his strategy. He had not wanted the struggle for control of the Western lands to escalate into open warfare, like fights among groups of common thieves. It would add nothing to his campaign for respectability.

It was now getting late, and Culver had been away from the party for too long. He stood, turned down the lights, and headed back to his guests.

Chapter 16

The moon shined brightly on the plank sidewalks of New Hope, casting shadows between the buildings. It was still early, but days were short this time of year.

O'Fallon's boots echoed on the wood as he made his way to the meeting of Quincy and Simpson, wondering if he had overplayed his hand. In the army, he had discovered that appearances were often more important than reality; a good bluff could often be more effective than any amount of raw strength or courage. O'Fallon, therefore, had invested most of his remaining savings in what otherwise would have been a foolish purchase: a new set of dress clothes that would have absolutely no value outside the city.

The suit was a little stiff, but was not uncomfortable. O'Fallon checked himself out in a shop window: gray wool suit, vest and coat, black tie. He was surprised that he did not feel or look out of place.

The face staring back at O'Fallon was not smiling. Rather, it showed little emotion. He was about to meet one of the most powerful men in the country, but he felt no excitement, no wonder. In the past several weeks, too much had happened, and his emotions were confusing. He often thought of Maria, a woman he barely knew and to whom he had no claim. He was having strange doubts about his thirst for revenge against Culver. The death of Hansen, and his decision to go after Braddock in search of Culver, which had almost gotten Quincy killed, left him with little taste for more killing. Yet, for years, his search for Culver had been the only thing that had kept him going; he had nothing now to replace the hate, so he continued to keep his emotions under tight control.

His eyes lost themselves in the shadows, and in spite of himself, O'Fallon thought of Maria. She had indicated on the trail to Parkersburg that she respected him and his search for the man that had killed his wife. What would she think if she saw him now? Would she see him in a different, more respectable light, or would she consider him as a man trying to be something he wasn't? When he had been with her, during the trip to Parkersburg, he had been dangerously close to feeling something other than pain, other than hate. He again tried to put the woman out of his mind, but the memories of her smiling at him from around the campfire would not go away.

O'Fallon half expected danger in the shadows, but the night remained quiet.

The store was still open, and the owner was watching O'Fallon through the glass. He stepped inside.

"Hello, sir," the owner said. "We were just getting ready to close up. How can I help you?"

"You have any pipes? And tobacco?" O'Fallon asked.

The owner displayed a selection on the counter. O'Fallon chose a medium-sized pot-bowl and some Kentucky burley. The purchase nearly depleted his remaining resources; he had only enough left for the evening. Normally, he would simply find a temporary job of some type to earn the few dollars he needed for supplies; now, however, he was so close to Culver, he didn't want to lose any more time, though he might not have any choice in the matter.

O'Fallon continued down the sidewalk, carefully packing the pipe so that it would break in properly. The pipe he had lost in the fight with Hansen had been with him since the army days; this pipe was a better one. The bowl burned cool, the aromatic smoke mixing with the night air. The air was chilly; the brisk wind was broken only by the buildings. The heels of his boots sent sharp vibrations through the boards. The sounds mingled with the other city noises.

O'Fallon emptied his pipe and entered the New Hope Hotel, where he was supposed to meet Quincy and Simpson. He spotted the two at a corner table; Simpson had his back to the wall. The restaurant was crowded, so O'Fallon had to step carefully through the mass of people, tables, chairs, and scurrying waiters. A few bumped into him, felt the steel of the Remington beneath his coat, looked at him strangely, but said nothing.

Quincy and his boss stood as O'Fallon reached the table. Quincy said, "Henry Simpson, Sean O'Fallon."

O'Fallon shook hands with Simpson, who said, "It's good of you to join us." His handshake was firm, his voice was warm. Neither he nor Quincy seemed surprised to see Sean in a suit. Both of them were dressed up, so O'Fallon decided he had made the right choice. He sat down and noted Simpson's appearance. He was a little over six feet and had wavy gray hair. His beard was white, well-trimmed, and joined with equally tailored sideburns. He seemed to be in his late forties or early fifties. His eyes were a cool gray.

Simpson began, "Did Josiah tell you why I traveled all the way from Chicago to meet you?"

"Only in general terms."

"Very well. We'll get to that later. Now, let's have dinner." He smiled. "It's my treat."

O'Fallon was vaguely uncomfortable at first. He felt out of his element, as if he were bluffing and would be called at any minute to show his hand. As the dinner progressed, however, he became more and more at ease. Simpson ordered wine for the party to go with the thick steaks.

"Progress! Progress!" Simpson was attacking his meal with enthusiasm. Enthusiasm was also in his voice, and it was almost contagious. "Progress is in the air! Miles of tracks are being laid into new territory every day. New buildings are going up. People are on the move, already looking to the next century. Who could have dreamed, even twenty years ago, that so much progress could be made in so short of a time!"

The excitement in Simpson's voice could not be contained. He was like some of the officers that O'Fallon had known: able to light a fire in even the dullest of men. Such officers were rare, but their presence often made the difference between victory or defeat.

"I've seen that progress myself," O'Fallon said. "Only a few weeks ago, I helped a man clear some land for a new town."

Simpson smiled and continued, "I always enjoy my trips West. It gives me a chance to see the progress being made. That's one reason why I made this trip myself. Why, last time I was here, this town was barely a wide spot in the road. And now look at it! The possibilities are endless!" He turned to Quincy, "What do you think, Josiah?"

"I agree, but I've had enough excitement for one year. In the past several days, I've been shot at, kidnapped, and nearly killed. I'll be glad to get back East, to a desk job again."

Simpson placed his fork neatly on his empty plate, daubed his lips with the napkin, and said, "Yes, I must thank you, Mr. O'Fallon, for protecting Mr. Quincy . . . and my interests." He pushed back from the table, pulled out a silver cigar case, and offered it to O'Fallon. Quincy took one, but Sean declined, pulling out his new pipe instead and filling it with tobacco.

"Gentlemen," Simpson said, "how about an after-dinner walk?"

As he stood, Simpson left twenty dollars on the table, which covered the meal plus a sizable tip.

The streets were still filled with people, but they were walking at a more leisurely pace. Many were wearing jackets, and a few had coats. Frost seemed to be in the air. The three men fell into step, with Quincy and Simpson puffing on their cigars and O'Fallon taking long draws on his pipe. After a few minutes, Simpson nodded slightly, and Quincy said, "Please excuse me, but I have some errands." Simpson

A COLD, DARK TRAIL   143

waved his hand in response, and Quincy puffed his way down the street into the crowd.

"Good man, that Quincy," Simpson said. "Damned fine engineer."

"He has a way of finding himself in tough spots."

"Yes, that's one of the things I wanted to talk to you about. I don't like to make mistakes in judgment, and, to be honest, I generally don't. This is one time I did. I knew that some others, besides myself, were interested in the territory. They didn't have the kind of connections and influence that I have, which allowed me to arrange approval for the survey and engineering study. As Quincy may have explained to you, that information is potentially very valuable. I never realized, however, that my competition would resort to murder and kidnapping. If you hadn't come along, Quincy would be dead and I'd be out of the services of a fine engineer and some very valuable information."

Simpson puffed on his cigar as he walked.

"It was a lucky coincidence that our paths crossed," O'Fallon said.

Simpson paused, leaned against a post.

"Quincy says you're a good man, and I believe him," Simpson said. "But I've looked into your background, and I'd say you're an extraordinary man. Your military record is flawless, full of commendations. You were wounded in battle, but instead of being a cripple, you're in better shape than some of my best men. You're quick. You're smart."

"I also can't be bought. What I'm doing, I'm doing for my own reasons."

"That's all right, as well. Being on the payroll is not for everybody. There is a lot to be said for being your own man."

The two started to walk again through the main business district, and were now strolling through the residential area. The houses were new, but tidy, and a few hardy late-summer flowers had yet to wither and die. A few kids were playing, away from the street.

"I had a long talk with Quincy, and the marshal, along with some of my other agents. I know that you and I are both working on the same side. We could help each other." O'Fallon continued smoking his pipe without comment. "Before you decide, let me tell you a little about our organization. We are, of course, a business. But we also have a dream that many of us share, that of progress. It is our destiny to expand, to grow, to meet the future with open arms."

"And in so doing, reap a profit."

"Of course." He paused, then said, "Quincy tells me your lady friend is a member of the Cherokee Nation. Without appealing to the self-interest in each of us, no progress could be made. Your lady friend, and many of the Cherokee leaders, understand this. They are considering leasing some land, selling other acres, for profit. They are sitting on untold wealth; eventually, this wealth will be exploited. The question is, By whom? And how? We are tough negotiators, but we are fair, and do not cheat anybody. You can be certain that the Cherokee people will receive far more from us for their land than from any other interested party. Especially men such as Winston Culver."

"What do you know about Culver?"

"Culver is a privateer who is trying to force his way into power using whatever means he has. He is ruthless and amoral. But he has planned his strategy well. He is buying his way into power using his ill-gotten gains."

"So what do you want from me?"

"I know you have a grudge against Culver; I'm not sure why, though I can guess. You and my organization could be a perfect marriage. You join our group, eliminate Culver, and we will assist you in every way we can, and pay you handsomely."

"The answer is still no. You're right; my fight is private, and is not for money."

Simpson sighed.

"Of course. Quincy said that would be your answer. And I respect your wishes. But I do have an alternative proposal for you."

"I'm listening."

"Quincy expected trouble, so he wisely left all his

notes and records at Parkersburg. He has made plans to retrieve them. But, as you noted, Josiah is not equipped to handle gunfighters and such. You, on the other hand, have proven yourself quite capable. We'd like for you to simply pick up the package for us.''

"And in return?"

"We'll pay you a generous one-time fee for services rendered. And we will also provide you with information that would lead you directly to Culver. What you do then is up to you. We cannot support you in any actions that the authorities might frown upon, you understand. We can, however, help to smooth any ensuing complications."

O'Fallon said, "Either way, I eliminate Culver for you, and I'd be working for you, not for myself. The answer is still no."

Simpson shrugged and responded, "Very well."

The two had now made an almost complete circle around the town, and had again entered the hotel bar. Quincy spotted them and hurried through the thinning crowd. He said, "Well, Sean? Are you going to accept Mr. Simpson's offer?"

"No."

Quincy's face suddenly drooped, and it looked as if the cigar would fall from his mouth.

"Not even to pick up the package from Maria? She's going to bring my notes and such, but I would sure feel better if you could join her. I don't think anybody would ever suspect her of making the delivery, but you never can tell."

O'Fallon tensed, then forced himself to calm down. He looked at Simpson and said, "You didn't tell me that Maria was involved."

"Oh? The Indian woman? Quincy didn't tell me the details of his plan. Would that influence your decision?"

The waiter brought the drinks that Quincy had ordered. O'Fallon held him away at arm's length as he stepped toward the surveyor. He said, "You set me up, you son of a bitch. You knew I couldn't abandon Maria once she got involved. I should have let them kill you."

Quincy backed up and said, shocked, "No, you have it all

wrong. The deal was set up before I realized how you felt about her. And it's true, I didn't tell Mr. Simpson about all my plans. I figured you'd help Maria in any case, but I wanted to give you a chance to join up with us first."

O'Fallon's hands fell to his side. The waiter placed the drinks in front of the men as if nothing had happened.

"Well, what is your decision?" Simpson urged.

"I'll retrieve your package, and make sure Maria makes it to New Hope safely," O'Fallon said. "That doesn't mean I'm your man."

Simpson smiled, raised his glass, and said, "Gentlemen, to the future!"

Chapter 17

The wind carried the smells of winter to O'Fallon: far-off snow, damp earth and grass, cold. Indian summer was over, and an early winter was fast approaching. O'Fallon had left his suit in New Hope, and was now wearing a sheepskin overcoat with the collar turned up to block the wind. The sky was gray and the air was clear.

O'Fallon had made good time, since he was traveling light. He had only enough rations for a week. His plan was to join Maria, deliver her and her package safely, and then be on his way to St. Louis. He was already in Indian Territory, and would soon be in Parkersburg. As the miles slipped by, he thought about how quickly a life can change.

The last time he had been in the territory, he'd had virtually no leads to Culver and little hope. Now, he had a direct connection to the renegade leader. Strangely, he also felt a faint stirring of anticipation. On the one hand, he hated the detour away from Culver, even one as brief as this one. On the other hand, he could not deny his eagerness to see Maria again. He was not sure why, since he still could not really imagine his life after he finally caught up with Culver. During the cold years of searching, he had not allowed himself to think about the future. Life had been simply getting through one day at a time, trying not to feel. Feeling was dangerous, opening himself to old ghosts and memories. But thinking about Maria was strange, and disquieting. And, for the first time in years, he thought maybe there might be hope after he achieved his revenge.

O'Fallon forced himself to concentrate on the situation at hand.

He paused at the top of a small rise to check out his surroundings. For some unknown reason, it seemed that Culver's group had given up on trying to get Quincy's information. Braddock, supposedly the local ringleader, had skipped town. And the men who had ambushed Quincy and Sean had also disappeared after their release from jail. O'Fallon didn't believe he was being followed. Still, a man couldn't be too careful.

Behind him, around him, the area was clear. The grass had turned brown with the frost and most of the leaves had fallen from the trees. In the distance, dark clouds rolled with the cold air. He spotted a small pack of wolves, which did not concern him. Later in the winter, when they were hungry enough, they could be dangerous. Now it was too early in the season, and their natural fear of men would keep them far away.

O'Fallon continued his ride along the old Indian trail. The wind grew sharper, even though the air remained clear, and O'Fallon could smell snow from the distant clouds. He would have to hurry to make Parkersburg before the storm hit. He hoped he would make it before Maria left. He did not want even a slight chance of her being exposed to Culver's men without protection.

About noon, he stopped again to check the trail. Once more, the land behind him was clear. This time he spotted a lone rider on the horizon in front of him. The figure was little more than a speck, and quickly dropped out of sight behind a hill. O'Fallon quickened his pace, but the rider was not seen again for the rest of the day.

The snow started to fall in the night. By morning, the ground had a light dusting of white. O'Fallon was up before dawn and on his way. As soon as it was light, O'Fallon turned off the path to higher ground.

The rider was back, and the figure was familiar. O'Fallon

A COLD, DARK TRAIL 149

smiled, shifted directions slightly to intercept the rider. He wasn't sure what he would say, or wanted to say. He forced himself to instead watch the trail.

The snow was coming down heavily when Sean's and Maria's paths finally intersected. O'Fallon pulled his horse beside the woman's and said, "Hello, Maria."

A brightly colored scarf protected her head and shoulders. Snow had covered the scarf. Maria did not seem surprised to see O'Fallon; instead she seemed pleased. Her smile was broad and genuine. To O'Fallon, she was just about the prettiest woman he had seen . . . since Laura. He had a sudden, insane urge to hug her.

Then he remembered where he was, and what he had to do. He held himself back, sitting quietly on the horse as snow fell around them. Maria sat easily on her own small horse. Her gear—and Quincy's valuable survey information—was packed in canvas bags tied behind the saddle.

"Hello, Sean." He had almost forgotten the music in her voice. She said, "I'm happy to see you again. I was afraid you might never stop running."

"I've never run from a fight."

"No, not from a fight." The snow was coming down heavier. The large flakes stuck to their clothes and the horses, forming an icy crust. "I knew you would come. Parker and some of the others had doubts. I'm glad you're here, instead of Quincy or one of Simpson's other men."

"So you know why I came back?"

"Of course."

Her smile was enigmatic.

O'Fallon heard some faint snarling in the distance. The sounds were carried by the wind, and he did not know how far away the wolves were. Perhaps they had found a prey. Or maybe one of the pack was rabid. The sounds distracted him slightly; they seemed out of place.

"You have Quincy's information."

"Yes. I'm glad you're here. Two men were asking a lot of questions in Parkersburg about you, me, Quincy. They followed me for a while outside of town." She pulled a small handgun from under her scarf. "A gift from Colin," she explained. "I was ready, but I'd rather you and I face them together."

"Do you know who the two men were?"

"They were locals named Bridger and Oxman—a couple of no-goods that have been in trouble with the Cherokee authorities and the federal government."

"I know them. Our paths have already crossed." O'Fallon frowned. He briefly considered tracking them down, but he did not want to leave Maria unprotected.

"I lost track of them a while back," Maria said. "I think they gave up."

"Then let's move on. Be careful."

The snow was coming down so heavily that the two could barely make out the path in front of them. The wind made talk difficult. Even though it was an early winter snow, drifts began to pile up.

"We should find shelter," Maria said. "We don't need to fight this snow."

"I saw no shelter coming in."

"You don't know the area as well as me." She pointed to the right. "There's an abandoned homestead not far from here. It would at least keep the snow out."

"Fine."

It wasn't more than an hour before the homestead came into view. The cabin and outbuildings were old. The barn was still standing, with some hay still in the loft. As they approached, O'Fallon said, "Go on inside. I'll take care of the horses—"

Suddenly wolves appeared from around the barn. The lead wolf was bleeding, just barely staying in front of the pack. Soon, the rest of the animals would be on the wounded leader. O'Fallon's horse laid its ears back. Maria's horse jumped in fright. She held on and kept the animal under control.

The lead wolf, in pain and anger, bared its teeth and jumped at O'Fallon. The man's hands were cold, but he still managed to draw his revolver and fire two shots in quick succession. The force of the heavy-caliber bullets stopped the animal in midleap. It fell to the ground, and the others almost immediately started to tear at its flesh. O'Fallon slid from his mount and grabbed its reins and those of Maria's horse.

In seconds, the two animals were inside the old barn. The structure was still relatively solid, so O'Fallon slammed the door behind them. Outside, the wolves were still snarling.

"They won't stay around long," Maria said. "This is a good shelter. Before the war, the family that lived here built this barn to last; they lost everything during the war."

The barn kept out most of the wind, and only a few small holes in the roof let in a dusting of snow. A loose door flapped back and forth in the hayloft. Sean climbed up, secured the door with its wooden latch. The interior was thrust into deeper shadows, and a sudden quiet. He threw hay down to the horses, and then some into one of the other compartments. He climbed down the ladder and got the bedrolls.

"What are you doing, Sean O'Fallon?"

"You need rest. I'm making you a place to stretch out."

"Sean, I'm not an invalid. I'm almost healed."

"Of course. I'm sorry."

"Don't be sorry. It's a sweet thought. And this is good protection from the weather."

Maria helped Sean pull down more hay and started to arrange it and the bedrolls. Outside, the wolves had sniffed around some more, and then slipped away into the woods. O'Fallon checked the doors, secured them. When he returned, Maria had completed her arrangements and had wrapped herself in a blanket. She said, "Come, sit with me."

O'Fallon spread the blankets around the two of them, and was surprised at the warmth. At first, O'Fallon felt clumsy and uncomfortable. One of the horses stomped its feet. Sean started to get up but was stopped by Maria's hand on his arm. He placed his heavy coat on top of the blankets and sat back down. Maria rested her head on O'Fallon's shoulder, and he slowly started to relax.

"I missed you, Sean."

O'Fallon listened to the wind blowing through the rafters and to the woman's soft voice. He didn't know how to reply without sounding silly. Finally, he said, "I thought a lot about you. I hoped to see you again."

The barn was quiet, then, except for the wind and the falling snow. It was not an uncomfortable silence. O'Fallon felt Maria's warmth and searched for the words, feeling clumsy and awkward again.

"I wanted to see you. I . . . enjoyed your company. But too much has happened. Since my wife, I haven't thought of much except . . ."

"Killing Culver."

"Yes," O'Fallon said, and the words sounded strange to him. "Once I loved. I dreamed of a family, a home. Those dreams were replaced with . . . something else. Hatred, I guess. I have nothing left to give."

Maria made a rude sound, startling Sean. She said, "That's stupid talk and you know it."

"I have nothing to give a woman like you. I mean, you're educated. You're cultured. You've been married to a powerful man and know what it's like to be a part of polite society. You have a home, and people that care for you."

"Sean, you're a brave and wonderful man, but you've been running from your feelings too long. I admire you for wanting to avenge your wife, but you've let it eat away at you. You haven't lost your humanity, your ability to feel and love. At least not yet. You've tried hard to convince yourself that all you have left is hate. You haven't yet succeeded."

Maria snuggled closer to O'Fallon and he found himself talking. He told the woman about all that had happened since he had left Parkersburg. He told about the attempts on his life, the difficult decisions he had faced—and how one of his decisions had almost cost Quincy his life. A part of him noted with amazement how easily he talked with her about his life, and how the more he talked the faster the words seemed to flow. It was like meeting with an old and dear friend after a space of many years: the closeness remained in spite of the distance, and there was so much to catch up on. It was also something more: a growing fire that did not threaten to consume him but to warm him, not an emptiness but a fulfillment. Maria nodded from time to time in understanding, squeezed his hand, and said nothing until his words finally started to slow.

"You try to act so tough, Sean O'Fallon," she said. "You try to act cold, and distant, but I know in your heart you're not that way. You stopped and saved my life, even at the risk of losing the trail to Culver. And, in the end, you did choose to help Quincy."

"And now I'm helping Simpson. I swore I would never work for another man. I was determined to find Culver on my own. It is my fight, and my fight only." He paused, looked Maria in the eye, and said, "I've been thinking about his offer. He's offering me Culver on a silver platter. Maybe I should accept. It would get me to Culver that much faster. What difference does it really make, anyway?"

"I can't answer that for you, Sean. You have to find your own peace. When my husband was killed, I responded to my grief differently than you. I ran away to lose myself in the land. I gave up my friends, and society, and almost gave up on life. Everybody urged me to return to town, to stop living by myself at the edge of the wilderness. It took a long time to heal." She touched O'Fallon lightly on his cheek. "Whatever your decision, I'm sure you will not lose yourself. You are a good man."

The woman snuggled closer under the blanket, and nothing more was said for the next hour. Night had fallen, and still Maria felt comfortable in Sean's arms. For the first time since before the war, he felt at peace. He didn't understand the feeling, and he did not question the feeling. The snow continued to fall softly. O'Fallon could hear it hitting the barn roof. Maria shifted position slightly, as did O'Fallon, and the emptiness in him turned to warmth.

O'Fallon pulled the woman gently to him and softly kissed her. She returned the kiss. A fire grew in O'Fallon that he thought had died long before.

Maria placed one hand around his neck and the other hand

inside his shirt. Maria's touch was a fire that warmed the winter night. Almost in spite of himself, O'Fallon moved closer and closer to the woman, losing himself to her warmth. . . .

He suddenly pulled back.

Maria said, "Sean?"

"Now's not the time," Sean said. "I want you too much, but not in this way. Later. After I take care of Culver. Maybe then we can be together, if you would have me."

Maria smiled and said nothing.

O'Fallon put his coat back on, said, "I'll be back in a few minutes. I just want to check outside."

The snow had covered the yard, the barn, and the surrounding hills. A light seemed to shine from everywhere and nowhere. He leaned against the old barn, watching the wind blow the snow into small drifts.

O'Fallon was puzzled. His doubts had grown, and killing Winston Culver no longer seemed to be the most important thing in his life. Suddenly, for the first time in years, he was starting to feel alive again. But he could not give up the fight now that he was so close. He stepped back inside, shook the snow off his coat, and joined Maria under the blankets. She was sleeping. She opened her eyes slightly when O'Fallon returned. He said, "I still have to get Culver. I still must avenge Laura."

If Maria heard, she did not let on. She rolled over, pressing her body fully against Sean.

He softly kissed the top of her head, arranged the covers better around her, and took her hand in his.

Outside, the snow continued to fall.

Chapter 18

Bridger had the hotel window cracked open in spite of the cold. He was leaning back in one of the chairs with his feet on the windowsill, watching the entrance of the New Hope Hotel. The early snow had melted quickly, leaving the streets even muddier than before. Most had chosen to stay inside.

"I'm getting tired of all this moving back and forth. I still don't understand why we hightailed it here, instead of taking the woman outside Parkersburg," Oxman said. He was sitting on the bed, picking mud out of his boots with his knife. "She was alone. It would have been easy."

"Yeah. Then we'd have to somehow get her out of the territory to St. Louis with O'Fallon on our asses. My plan is better. The five-thirty P.M. train is the last one out for twenty-four hours; we'll take her, and be on the train and in St. Louis before O'Fallon knows what hit him. He'll follow us—but a day later, on our terms. By the time he gets to us, we'll be ready to bring him down in front of Braddock and Culver." Oxman shrugged. Bridger said, "Read me back that letter I dictated."

Oxman returned the knife to its sheaf, picked up the letter from the bed, shook off some specks of dried mud, and read: " 'O'Fallon you dumb bastard we got your woman and give her to Culver. We gonna kill you.' "

"That should bring him running," Bridger said, smiling.

"I'm kind of glad now that your mom learned you how to write."

Oxman placed the paper in his pocket. "I don't know about this," he complained. "I'm not even sure Culver is interested in O'Fallon. From what Lancer told us, it seems like Braddock and Culver were more interested in the information that surveyor had. I think maybe we'd be better off forgetting about O'Fallon and the girl and going after—"

Bridger pulled his gun without looking at the other man and placed it on the windowsill. He said, "You're not backing out on me now, are you?"

"No . . . no."

"Just leave that letter with the clerk after I get the woman. O'Fallon will follow us, and then we'll have him." He flexed his fingers around the gun handle, then returned the revolver to the holster. "You've already arranged things with the clerk?"

"He's got the money. He'll let us know where to find them." Oxman gestured out the window to the street, almost in disbelief. "Look at that," he said. "You were at least right about them coming straight to the hotel when they got back to town."

Below, O'Fallon and Maria rode along the edge of the muddy street, stopping in front of the New Hope Hotel. O'Fallon helped Maria from the horse. He lifted her gently over the mud to the wooden sidewalk. He removed the canvas packs and followed her toward the building.

"Well, a gentleman," Bridger said. "That whore *would* pick somebody who thinks he's a hot piece of shit. We'll see how tough he is when we steal the woman and bring him down in front of Culver. We'll give them a few minutes to settle down. Remember, I get to take care of the woman." He pulled out his watch. "We'll soon be on our way."

O'Fallon glanced up and down the street, but saw nothing suspicious. He was surprised that they had not been followed and had experienced no problems returning to New Hope. It made him nervous. Several times he had taken a chance and left Maria alone so that he could circle around and check out his back trail, but he had found nothing. Apparently the men following Maria from Parkersburg had changed their minds.

O'Fallon watched Maria walk across the plank sidewalk, and felt lighter than he had felt in many years. He covered the same ground in a few long steps and held the door open for her. She smiled.

The two stepped into the lobby. The clerk said, "Mr. Simpson is expecting you. He is in the dining room."

"Relax," she said. "Looks like your friends are here."

"Not friends," he said. They entered the dining room. Simpson and Quincy stood and greeted the couple. Quincy shook their hands.

"How was your trip?" Simpson said.

"Uneventful," O'Fallon said.

"Good! Good," Simpson said.

O'Fallon handed the canvas bags to Quincy, who was smiling at Maria. He said, "I don't mean to be rude, Mr. Simpson, but I've filled my end of the bargain."

"And I'll fill mine, make no mistake about it. I can be of the greatest help to you, if you would let me. I hope you thought about my offer over the past several days."

Quincy raised the canvas bags and said, "I'm going to put these in the safe."

Simpson dismissed him with a wave of his hand. O'Fallon remained standing. He said, "I'm still not interested."

"I'll give you the information you seek. I'll tell you exactly where to find Winston Culver. You've earned that already." He paused, then added, "Even better, I'll deliver you to his doorstep and provide what assistance I can. What would you need? Horses? Explosives? More men? Protection from the law? I can provide them all."

O'Fallon glanced at Maria. Her face was impassive. O'Fallon said, "The answer's still no."

Simpson shook his head. "You are a very stubborn man, Mr. O'Fallon, rejecting an offer of employment that many men can only dream about. You have my respect, however. Men of character are rare, which makes them so valuable."

He sighed, reached into his pocket, and pulled out an envelope. "My information—the best money can buy—is that Winston Culver is spending virtually all of his time in his nearly completed office building. Here are the directions, as promised. Also in the envelope is the payment for your successful completion of your assignment—and a bonus."

O'Fallon took the envelope, and opened it to reveal a wad of green, a sheaf of plain paper covered with neat writing, and a train ticket. Simpson pulled out a gold pocket watch from his vest.

"I knew you would want to waste no time, so I took the liberty of providing a ticket on the next train to St. Louis, scheduled to leave in less than two hours. If you would like, I could make that two tickets . . ."

"No, one is enough."

Maria started to protest, but O'Fallon answered, "I hate leaving you, but this is something I must do on my own."

"I would like to be with you. I . . ."

"This is something I must do on my own," O'Fallon said firmly. Maria hesitated, finally saying nothing.

"Now that Simpson has Quincy's engineering notes, you'll be safe. Stay here, and I'll be back for you. I promise."

O'Fallon kissed her, trying to memorize the feeling of her body against his, the touch of her hair against his cheek. He had said so many good-byes in his life, he wondered if he would ever be able to find an end to his search. He stuffed the envelope in his shirt and was gone.

Maria's eyes softly followed him through the door until he was lost in the growing crowd.

The crowd had started to gather in the late afternoon. Bridger and Oxman were rough-looking, but blended with the pulsating masses. Oxman watched through the large window in the front of the hotel as Quincy had the clerk place a few canvas bags in the safe. Oxman quickly slipped back into the crowd when O'Fallon started toward the door. The two Indians waited in the background until the lobby had cleared temporarily. Oxman moved to the desk, talked with

A COLD, DARK TRAIL

the clerk, and made a few quick signs to Bridger, who started up the stairs.

He moved quietly down the hall until he came to Maria's room. He took a quick glance around and then tried the knob.

The door was locked.

Bridger kicked out and the door splintered around the knob. Bridger rushed into the room, moving his body down and to the right in case Maria had a gun.

The woman was standing at the washbasin, reaching for her gun. It was no more than three feet away, but it did her no good.

"Hello, Maria," Bridger said. "Remember me?" He kicked the gun away, but Maria was already reaching into her bag. "Uh-huh. None of that." He grabbed her wrist, twisted, and swept the bag from the bed. He pulled his gun and said, "You're coming with me."

"You dirty lowlife scum—"

Bridger hit the woman on the side of the head with the barrel of his gun, and she fell across the bed. Bridger examined her. A huge bump had already formed, but she would live. Bridger almost never made that kind of mistake.

He ripped the bedsheets into strips, tied her hands and legs and stuffed more strips into her mouth. He pulled out a large burlap bag and quickly stuffed her into it. They would be riding in the baggage section, where such a package would hardly be suspicious.

The whole operation had taken less than five minutes.

He tossed the bag over his shoulder, listened at the door, and then slipped out as quietly as he had entered. This would be the most difficult part: to get out of the hotel without being seen.

He made it almost to the stairs without incident. Just before he got to the steps, however, he heard a voice and then footsteps. He tried the first door he came to. It was unlocked, so he opened it and went inside.

A satchel was on the bed.

Bridger waited, listening to the bootsteps walking up the

stairs. He hoped the man would keep going. This was a simple operation. He didn't need complications.

The doorknob turned. The door opened. The man stepped through, and Bridger slammed him hard with his fist. Bridger hit him harder than he intended. He heard bone crack, and the man fell in a lifeless mass.

Bridger shrugged and dumped Maria on the floor with a thump. He dragged the man into the room and rolled him under the bed. He was still breathing, but he would be out for hours, at least. By then Bridger would be safely on his way to St. Louis.

He grabbed Maria and again stepped into the hallway. This time he was lucky and made it down the stairs without incident. He waved to Oxman and left through the back door.

Oxman placed the remaining cash on the counter. The clerk picked up the money, and then froze as he felt Oxman's knife pricking into his belly.

"Oh, yeah, one more thing before I leave," he said. "Open the safe."

"Wait a minute. That wasn't part of the deal. You just wanted a couple of room numbers."

"Open the safe or I'll kill you."

The clerk quickly turned and in seconds the safe was opened. Oxman stuffed jewelry and cash in his pockets, then grabbed the canvas packs.

"What am I going to tell Mr. Simpson?"

Oxman shrugged. His knife flashed upward and sideways. The clerk crumpled behind the counter, shiny blood pooling on the floor from the long slit in his neck. Oxman took the money from the clerk's hands, returned it to his own pocket. He pulled the letter out, smiled, tore it into pieces, and tossed it into a nearby spittoon.

"Bridger can have the woman," he muttered. "The information is what Culver really wants. I don't want O'Fallon following us at all."

The train would be leaving in minutes. In less than twenty-four hours, Oxman figured, he would be a rich man.

* * *

At the station, Simpson made one final attempt.

"Join my organization, and I'll make you field head of security over all my Western interests," he said. "You can name your salary."

The train pulled into the station, the dirty steam graying the already dusky air.

"Sorry, no."

"Well, then, I would like to suggest some ideas, and make an offer of assistance."

Quincy was no longer with his boss, who now had a number of other aides looking at O'Fallon sourly.

"I'll listen to your ideas," Sean said.

Simpson reached up, and an aide placed a cigar in his hand. One of the bodyguards lit the cigar. Simpson said, "Culver came from a poor background. His mother was a whore, and he grew up in the streets of Charleston. During the war he made a name for himself and enough money to live comfortably for many years. But that wasn't enough for him. What he craves most is respect. Power. He is using his money to buy that respectability. He may eventually even buy his way into the Senate."

"All that means nothing to me," O'Fallon said.

"Maybe not. I don't know what your dreams of vengeance have been. Perhaps you had visions of facing him, man-to-man, and slugging it out. Forget all that for a minute. Think about what would hurt him the most: a blow to his hard-won respectability. I know the way to accomplish this. He just completed a new building on the St. Louis riverfront as a symbol to the world that he is a power to reckon with. Wouldn't you like to bring it down around his ears? I looked into your record. You know your way around explosives. You could do it."

Simpson's voice was now slow, measured, almost hypnotic. O'Fallon almost smiled at the thought of Culver's building crashing down around him.

"It could be done, even without a whole lot of powder, if I set the charges right. . . ."

"I will arrange to have the resources made available to

you on your arrival. Obviously, I cannot support you openly, though I can guarantee you won't get caught. Fires are quite common in the downtown area, so nobody would suspect anything out of the ordinary. And I have a great many friends in the city."

"If it's so easy, why not do the job yourself?"

"I'm not a common criminal. I don't deal with my enemies through violence. I also know the world is not black and white, and am not above helping another person achieve his ends when they correspond to mine."

O'Fallon knew the answer was a lie. He started to reject the offer, but then he thought of his wife, raped and killed by Culver's gang during the war, and the lie suddenly seemed irrelevant.

"Make the resources available as you will. I may use them, or I may not. I have to think about it."

Simpson smiled broadly, as if the matter were already settled.

Chapter 19

The train moved at a speed O'Fallon had never thought possible. The others in the first-class coach, however, seemed to take it all in stride. Sean figured they were mainly business travelers, used to the modern technology. One sat quietly, smoking cigars and reading a newspaper. Another was going over what looked like legal papers. Others leaned back in the plush seats, legs crossed. All were dressed very well.

It was dark, but not yet so late that the passing countryside could not be seen, though to O'Fallon it seemed mainly a blur of browns and grays.

In some ways, O'Fallon felt as if his life had become part of the scenery outside the train: blurred, passing too quickly for understanding. In a matter of weeks, he had gone from being an almost penniless drifter with only a faint hope for vengeance to traveling in first-class luxury to the very doorsteps of the man he had pledged to kill. When Sean had made the oath to destroy Culver, back in Tennessee at his wife's grave, he had not imagined the end coming this way.

O'Fallon liked Quincy all right, but he seemed a little naive about the nature of the man he was working for. O'Fallon did not trust Simpson or his organization. He knew that even now, he was also helping Simpson, helping him fulfill his own arcane plans and goals. O'Fallon planned to kill Winston Culver for personal reasons, but in so doing he would also eliminate one of Simpson's business competitors. No wonder Simpson was so anxious to help! Yet, Simpson was finally leading him to Culver. Accepting his help didn't mean O'Fallon was no longer his own man.

Or did it?

If Sean accepted Simpson's offer of employment, he would probably have more money and power than he had ever imagined. The problem was, he did not want that for his life. After this mess was over—if he could walk away from it—he planned to have no further contact with Culver, Simpson, or anything even remotely related to their dirty businesses. All he wanted now was . . .

Maria.

The feelings were strange. He had loved Laura, back in Tennessee. He remembered the sunshine, the hills, their marriage night. Maria was totally different from Laura, and the feelings were different. Yet, they were there just the same. He felt at peace with Maria, and happy, and warm. With her, he believed there would be life, and love, and hope. After all the years of cold darkness, she was almost too good to be true.

Maybe, possibly, he could persuade Maria to join him after this mess was over. He had refused to seriously consider such a possibility, in spite of the night in the barn. For one thing, he might not live past his revenge on Culver; if he had to sacrifice himself to bring down his enemy, he would do so. Too, any kind of emotion other than hate was still relatively new and strange to O'Fallon, and he could not afford to indulge in dreaming about what might never come to pass. He had to keep his wits about him now more than ever.

He tried to push the thoughts of the woman to arm's length, to consider his next move.

From time to time a touch of white could be seen, mixed with the greens and browns and grays. Apparently the snowstorm had passed quite a ways to the east, and had left patches on the ground in shaded pockets.

The metal wheels clanked against the rails. The smell of leather from the seats filled the coach.

Simpson had said Culver would probably be in his new

office building on the riverfront. O'Fallon wanted to kill Culver, face-to-face, and let him know why he was dying. It would also be appropriate to bring the man's new building down around him.

O'Fallon leaned back in his seat, tilted his hat over his face, and tried to rest, though the dreams of Laura, Maria, the war, the burned cabin, and Culver continued to mix hopelessly in his mind.

Bridger and Oxman had lowered the bag enough for Maria's head to stick out. She had worked herself upright, and as far from the two men as possible, though when she had tried to move beyond the horses Bridger had caught her, slapped her a few times, and tossed her back to her original position.

The wheels were noisy and the car swayed back and forth, threatening to bounce the men into the horses.

"Dammit, Bridger, couldn't you have found something better than this?"

"The damned train was getting ready to leave. I had to find a place fast, where nobody would find us. Maybe I should have checked us—all three of us—into first class. What a fine idea that would be." He scratched himself, stretched his legs with his back to the wall. "This stock car is good enough."

"Nothing like smelling like horse shit when we meet up with Braddock," Oxman said, moving the canvas sacks away from soiled hay that one of the animals had kicked up. "Make a helluva impression."

"When they see what we brought them, it won't make no difference what we smell like. You think O'Fallon's got the letter yet? Wouldn't you like to see his face when he finds out we got his woman and are taking her to his oldest enemy!"

"You know, O'Fallon may have other things on his mind. It may be days . . . weeks . . . before he gets the letter. If ever."

"But that would mess up the plan!"

Oxman pulled the canvas bags closer to him and said, "We'll see how it plays when we get to St. Louis."

In St. Louis, Culver said, "What do you think?"

Braddock picked up the telegram from his desk. His office was located in Culver's new building on the Mississippi riverfront.

"I don't like it," Braddock said. "Bridger and Oxman are lowlife Cherokees. They used to work for one of my ex-agents, who proved to be so incompetent that I had to get rid of him. Any scheme they have has to be half-assed."

"Maybe. Maybe not. Apparently they were able to obtain the survey information that you could not."

Braddock reddened.

"They shouldn't have brought the woman."

Culver leaned back in his chair and watched Braddock's face with mild amusement. "What does the woman have to do with this business?"

"Probably nothing."

Culver held the telegram close to the gas lamp and read:

> We have the information. We have Maria Rushing. Arrival early train.

"Rushing . . . the name sounds familiar." Culver snapped his fingers. "I remember now. Jim Rushing was one of those agitators during the war. He almost kept the Cherokee Nation neutral in the war. Wasn't he the one you had killed?"

"So the woman is Jim Rushing's wife. It doesn't mean anything now."

"Is she pretty?"

"If you like Indian women."

Culver tapped the telegram as he thought.

"The survey information is valuable. It could save me years of work and expense. In the end, though, it is just facts and figures. This woman might be able to add information of a different sort. Various key people who might help smooth our way, others who might cause us problems and need to be eliminated. She can place the facts and figures in context. Wives of politicians often know more about these matters than we give them credit for."

Braddock reddened again. "There is nothing wrong with the intelligence I have been providing you."

"No. Of course not. You've done a good job. That's why you're still with the organization. That's why I brought you here, to work with me. Still, it never hurts to double-check your information." He folded the telegram and returned it to Braddock. "Besides, this woman might provide a pleasant diversion for me."

"I don't like it," Braddock said. "Let me call in a few extra men."

"No need. This building is secured. I have several guards positioned outside the building. In any case, I think we want as few witnesses as possible while I . . . question . . . the woman." He smiled. "I'm glad I had the foresight to include an apartment for my use in the building. It will make things quite handy for me. Being this near the river will make disposal of her body easy. I'm sure that these two—Bridger and Oxman—would be more than happy to complete the work for me."

Culver's laughter echoed hollowly through the halls of the new building.

Chapter 20

Bridger and Oxman moved slowly through the back alley in the wagon. Maria sat between them, her hands tied and her mouth gagged. The canvas bag containing Quincy's notes was at Oxman's feet.

The night had turned cold and drizzly. A heavy fog had moved in from the Mississippi. The streets were deserted except for a few late-night drinkers. The Culver Building could be seen faintly through the mist.

"We made it," Bridger said. "I still don't know why you had to go and steal those bags from the safe. I thought for sure that would jinx the plan."

"The timing was perfect. We were out of the city before the clerk's body was even found. And who could tie us into the theft? It may bring us a little extra money or something."

Maria struggled again, but her words were muffled through the gag. Bridger backhanded her, snapping her head back. She glared at him, but stopped straining against her bonds. Bridger laughed, and said, "You sure are a feisty bitch. Try it again. I'd enjoy it if you tried to get away." The wagon creaked over the rough street. The sound echoed in the cold night. "What was it you said in that telegram?" Bridger asked.

"Not much. Just that we had the information and the woman."

"Did you mention the fact that O'Fallon will also be on

his way? That we've got his woman and that we can set a trap for him."

The wagon had now pulled up to the door. Oxman said, "Well, here we are. Let's go on inside. They're expecting us."

Bridger stopped the wagon, pulled the hand brake, and picked up Maria from the seat.

Oxman tried the door. It was unlocked and opened silently on well-oiled hinges. The two stepped inside, Bridger carrying the woman and Oxman the canvas bag. Faint light from outside cast faint shadows through the plate-glass window facing the street to the front office area. Braddock was standing at the other end of the room with his arms crossed. A gaslight shined in the hall behind him next to the staircase.

"So you idiots finally made it," he said.

"Hey! You can't talk to us like that. . . ."

"Shut up." Braddock uncrossed his arms and stepped toward the two men. "You two are even more stupid than your ex-boss, Lancer. What are you trying to pull?" He paused, cocked his head, and said deliberately, as if it corroborated his point, "Besides, you smell like shit."

Bridger said angrily, "You should be glad to see us. We got O'Fallon's woman. He'll probably be here tomorrow. In the meantime, we can set up the trap for him. . . ."

Braddock's glare silenced the other man.

"What's the idea of leading O'Fallon here? He's been nothing but trouble for me, and now you bring him straight to me. I am dealing with a couple of empty-headed fools!"

Bridger started to reach for his gun. Oxman stopped him and said, "Don't worry about it. O'Fallon thinks Maria is still safe in New Hope. He doesn't know about her kidnapping."

"Yeah? What about that letter we wrote. . . ." Bridger said.

"I tore it up," Oxman said. "I thought it was best. O'Fallon will never get the letter, and never suspect we have the woman."

"You did what?" Bridger said. "That wasn't the plan! I should—"

Braddock interrupted him. "I'm glad one of you has a little sense. Your telegram said you have the survey information. Did you by any chance bring it? Or is that too much to expect?"

Oxman held out the bag. Braddock took it, and then ungagged Maria. Her face was puffy and bruised. Her eyes still blazed fire.

"Well, you don't look too bad," Braddock said. "What do you know about the engineering survey?"

"Go to hell."

"Yeah. Culver will like dealing with you. What's with this O'Fallon character? Who is he? What is he after?" Braddock walked around her. "Are you really his woman? What will he do when he gets to St. Louis and finds your body floating in the river?"

Maria didn't answer.

"Well, they're rhetorical questions, anyway." He untied her and said, "Culver wants to talk with you." He reached out, pulled Maria to him, and then toward the door leading into the building. Her hand struck out. He slapped her to the floor, then pulled her back to her feet. Bridger laughed. Braddock said, "You two stay out of the way."

"What about a reward or something?" Bridger asked. "We'd like to join your organization."

"You did all right, in spite of your stupidity. Maybe we can find a place for you. You stay here while I deliver this to Culver. Then maybe we'll talk."

He left the room, leaving the two men in silence.

"Son of a bitch," Bridger said, under his breath.

"We pulled it off," Oxman said. "I hated to cross you, but it turned out for the best."

"Hey, no hard feelings!" Bridger said. He pulled a bottle from his coat pocket, took a seat in one of the chairs. He placed his feet on a desk and motioned to Oxman to join him. "We're here, might as well relax. Have a couple of swigs. To celebrate, you might say."

Oxman took the bottle, but cautioned, "I'm not sure what Culver would say about you resting those boots on his new desk."

"Don't worry about it. We're part of the organization now!"

Oxman took another drink, then handed the bottle back to the bigger man.

The cold seemed to soak through O'Fallon's heavy coat into his bones. The bed of the wagon he was driving was covered in waterproof canvas to protect the explosives from the weather and any curious passersby. At three-thirty A.M., however, the streets were deserted. He had all the tools and power needed to destroy Culver's building, courtesy of Simpson.

O'Fallon had been surprised when one of Simpson's men met him at the station with the wagon. Sean had lifted the tarp to reveal the tools and powder. The other man simply handed over the reins and said, "Compliments of Mr. Simpson."

The fog had turned to drizzle as O'Fallon traveled across the deserted roads from the station to Culver's new building, following the directions that Simpson had provided to him. Many of the roads were familiar from his convalescence in the city following the war. He remembered how his love for his wife had kept him moving during that time, in spite of the pain, until he could walk again. He remembered the hate he had felt after he had found Laura dead in Tennessee, and how it had kept him moving during the next terrible years. His hate had carried him over many miles since those times. Had it taken him so far that he could now casually destroy a building and risk innocent lives?

O'Fallon had never considered himself that kind of a man. During the war, he had used explosives. After the war, he had killed too often. He had never liked the killing, though he had long anticipated a pleasure at killing Culver. That time was now close. The long, cold trail would soon reach its end.

O'Fallon glanced at the tarp-covered wagon bed, and asked himself again, Is this what I really want to do? In the past weeks he had come close to becoming a man he never wanted to be. He had come close to being no better than Culver or his thugs.

He continued his slow ride to the building.

He stopped the wagon several hundred feet behind Culver's building. He wanted to take a closer look at the site before he decided any other action.

O'Fallon walked quietly along the wet back alley, his boots barely splashing the shallow puddles. He circled around the deserted streets, staying in the shadows, until he could gain a clear view of the front of the building. It was an impressive brick structure with a large, plate-glass front window. Modern gaslights provided illumination from two of the offices on the second floor. O'Fallon saw movement through the window. He changed positions, still staying in the shadows, to get a better view. He recognized two Indians—Bridger and Oxman—drinking from a common bottle in the front lobby.

He suddenly felt a presence at his back. Without pausing, he pivoted and smashed his fist against the face of the man behind him. The man crumpled. O'Fallon rolled him over. The man was dressed in expensive, fashionable clothes but had the muscles of a fighter. Sean dragged him from the street.

There would be more guards. O'Fallon started to carefully search the shadows for the other men so that he could get on with his work.

Maria stepped through the door in front of Braddock. She held her body erect, even though it was stiff and sore. Her face, puffy and bruised, remained impassive. Bridger had had quite a bit of fun with her in the stock car on the way to St. Louis. Still, she was of a leading Cherokee family, and she was not going to show weakness.

She recognized Braddock as one of the corrupt government men who had been in office prior to the war. Now, he was apparently working for Culver. It figured.

Culver was sitting at his desk. The room was lit with gaslights. Nothing but the newest and best would be used by this up-and-coming businessman. The building was so new that it still smelled of fresh wood and paint.

Braddock smiled and said, "Winston Culver, Maria Rushing."

Culver stood, offered his hand, and said, "Welcome. Please. Have a seat."

His voice was deep, calm, and he had a charming way about him. His eyes, however, were hard. Maria remained standing and did not offer her hand in return. Culver laughed and sat back down. He leaned back in his leather chair and folded his hands together. The light seemed to make his gray hair stand out from the dark paneling. He was still fairly young, but he already looked like a distinguished politician.

"I understand your boyfriend has been causing some problems for my organization," Culver said. Maria remained silent. "I consider him only a minor annoyance, at best," Culver continued. "As you know, we obtained the information we sought, in spite of O'Fallon's best efforts. I understand you also have much knowledge about the situation in the Cherokee Nation. Perhaps your information could also be valuable? Why don't you relax, and we'll become better acquainted." He motioned to Braddock and added, "Leave us alone, now. I can handle this."

Braddock shrugged and started for his own office, located down the hall. He left Culver's door open a fraction of an inch.

Maybe it was fatigue, or disbelief that he had finally found Culver, or an unwillingness to accept the nature of his actions, but Sean moved as if in a dream. His superior instincts and skills, honed by his years in the mountains of Tennessee, allowed him to make short work of the guards. He continued to move cautiously, and his senses remained alert, but he felt somehow detached.

He tried the loading dock entrance, which led into the basement area of the building. The door was unlocked and opened quietly.

This section of the new building was still empty; even though Culver had moved his offices in, full-fledged operations had not yet started. Some of the building materials remained in piles, awaiting final cleanup. A few structural supports remained exposed. O'Fallon quickly, skillfully, set the charges, but was surprised to remain so emotionally apart from the work. Why was he doing this? Still, he continued to work, almost by instinct, twisting the lengths of fuse together.

The large basement area was deathly quiet. O'Fallon checked his work one final time, but did not light the fuse. That would be the last action taken, the final act of vengeance after O'Fallon had looked Culver in the eye, told him why he was going to die, and then killed him.

Or was the hesitancy the result of some deeper doubt?

O'Fallon suddenly heard voices coming through the door at the top of the stairs. He moved against the far wall.

The voices stopped, leaving the room even quieter than before.

Chapter 21

Bridger and Oxman had half emptied the bottle when Bridger said, "What's that?"

"I didn't hear anything."

"From downstairs. I think somebody's down there."

Oxman took another drink. He said, "It's probably one of Culver's guards."

Bridger took the bottle and another drink.

"And what if it isn't?"

"It's not our problem. Who do you think it might be? O'Fallon?" Oxman laughed. "How could he know you got the woman? And even if he knew, how could he get here so soon? The next train out of New Hope isn't until tomorrow."

"Yeah. But we're part of Culver's group now. I didn't see any other guards around when we walked in. I think we should check it out."

Oxman took another sip and slipped the bottle into his pocket.

"Maybe you're right. It doesn't hurt to be careful. It'll show Braddock how valuable we can be."

The two walked into the hall. Bridger motioned toward the stairs leading to the bottom floor, sensing movement in the shadows. Without speaking, the two men slipped into different offices on either side of the hall.

* * *

O'Fallon slowly, softly walked up the stairs and opened the door into the hall. The building remained quiet, but O'Fallon's keen eyes scanned the darkness for any sign of danger.

He moved cautiously forward, listening. He heard the voices again, and recognized them as the two Indians who had attacked him and had been asking about him and Maria at Parkersburg. There were many rooms leading from the hall, which ended at the main entrance. Which room were they in?

The Remington was in his hand, but Sean did not want to use the gun just yet. The sound would alert Culver and ruin the surprise entrance that O'Fallon had planned.

Sean had rehearsed his speech in his mind for days. He would calmly explain to Culver why he had to die. It would be simple, surgical. And after it was all over, O'Fallon would retire his revolver, and leave behind his life of hate. He hoped that Maria would join him.

If he lived through the night.

O'Fallon took a step, another step, and then froze. Two men were coming toward him from the front of the building. Sean pushed himself against a wall, and the other two men also disappeared.

The hall was dark, except for the faint light coming through the front door. O'Fallon knew patience, and he waited. Five minutes, then ten minutes, passed. Finally, one of the men moved. It was only a slight rustling of cloth, but it was enough to give away the other man's location. O'Fallon moved stealthily down the hall to gain better position.

Even tiny sounds seemed amplified in the dark building. Sean heard a slight creak. He dived to the floor just as the door to his right flew open. A shot fired from the doorway. The sound filled the hall. The bullet hit the wall near O'Fallon. Chunks of plaster stung his arm.

He rolled to the doorway where the shots had been fired. He stood, stepped inside. Oxman shot, shot again, and then exited through another room to the rear. O'Fallon gave chase as another shot was fired from the door behind him. Sean returned the fire, causing Bridger to fall back into the hall. O'Fallon followed Oxman into an adjoining office.

Oxman was moving along the wall in the darkness. Sean could hear the other man moving cautiously, and placed Oxman's location. He said, "Hold it right there."

The renegade spun around, shot, and then dropped to the floor. Again he shot wildly in the dark. O'Fallon had now started around the other side of the room.

Oxman slowly got to his knees, warily scanning the darkness.

O'Fallon moved to within inches of the Indian and placed the gun barrel next to the other man's side. Oxman moved quickly, but not fast enough. He turned, shot. The bullet missed Sean by inches and caused O'Fallon's own shot to go slightly off the mark. Still, the slug tore through Oxman's skin and muscle to exit from the other side of the body. The Indian tried to run, but his legs gave out from under him. He hit the floor, made one final shot. The hammer hit an empty chamber. O'Fallon held his shot, and said, "Where's Culver?"

Oxman moved his left hand toward O'Fallon. A knife suddenly appeared in his right hand. The Indian slashed out, cutting through the front of O'Fallon's coat and shirt. Sean fired. The bullet hit the Indian in the chest. He collapsed to the floor. The knife fell from Oxman's hand with a clatter. The blood spread quickly from the wounds across the hardwood floor. The Indian opened his mouth. O'Fallon moved cautiously closer.

"Damned if you didn't find out about the woman, anyway," the Indian said. O'Fallon froze, a chill running through him colder than any winter wind. "No matter. Culver's got her."

"You lie."

Oxman laughed, and died, the blood bubbling from his mouth.

The Tennessee man crouched in a dark corner by the door to reload his gun. He knew Bridger was near, but did not know his exact location. O'Fallon cocked the weapon and then slipped back into the dark hall.

Braddock had left the door to Culver's office open a crack so he could be available if trouble broke out. He wasn't sure what kind of trouble to expect. The woman had been pretty well beaten into submission, and Culver had much experience in handling feisty ladies. The two Indians who had brought her in were too stupid to cause much trouble.

What about O'Fallon?

That man had single-handedly destroyed the operation that Braddock had been putting together in Indian Territory. He had killed some very tough characters, and had come out of it apparently unharmed. Still, there was no way he could cause a problem to Culver's organization—not at the home base in St. Louis. There was no way that O'Fallon could be in St. Louis so soon. Or was there? Maybe he had more powerful friends than Culver realized? Braddock made plans to post more guards the following morning, regardless of Culver's wishes. He wished Culver would have let him bring in a few extra men tonight, as well. Culver was brilliant, but sometimes too stubborn.

As for Maria, Braddock had no feelings one way or the other. She was an Indian woman who had the bad luck to be in his way, just as her husband had been years before. Braddock knew that Culver still enjoyed some rough sport in spite of his polished veneer. He would have his fun with the woman, then get rid of her. It would be a simple matter.

The next question was what to do about the two Indians. Culver might even be foolish enough to give them jobs, in appreciation for bringing him the woman. He had awarded his gunfighter, Jack Hansen, for similar efforts during the war. Braddock had killed Lancer easily enough; however, it might not be so easy to kill both of the Indians together.

Braddock sat down at his desk. His office was located near Culver's. The screams hadn't started yet, so Culver was apparently still setting the woman up. Or maybe she was just too beaten to scream.

A COLD, DARK TRAIL

He shrugged and moved a stack of papers to one side.

The first shot echoed through the building like an explosion. Braddock moved fast. Almost instantly he was out from behind his desk, gun in hand. The next shots sounded quickly, broken by brief periods of silence. Braddock got to the hall just as the door to Culver's office opened. The gaslight shined almost like a halo around Culver's handsome profile.

"What the hell's going on?" he demanded.

"Get back in the office, and have your gun ready. I'm looking into it."

Culver paused, but his face was in shadow. He turned without further comment, closing the door behind him.

Instinctively, Braddock knew it was O'Fallon.

Braddock didn't know how the man could be in St. Louis, in the middle of Culver's building, unless he was working for Simpson, after all. The shots were not near Culver's office, so apparently the two Indians had found him and given fight. Maybe he would at least take care of the problem of the two Indians. Braddock doubted if they would last long against O'Fallon.

Braddock knew the building better than O'Fallon, however, which might give him the advantage.

He turned down the gaslight and went in search of the man from Tennessee.

Sean felt a presence behind him, and stepped out of the way as Bridger shot. The bullet missed O'Fallon, and the Indian ran from the room, firing a shot behind him. Sean shot once at the running figure, but missed. He moved carefully down the hall.

The element of surprise was gone. One of the guards was dead. That left Bridger, and who else? He had gotten past three outside guards. How many were on the inside? He opened each door as he came to it. The offices were all richly furnished, though vacant. Simpson had said the building was very new. Judging by the number of offices, Culver apparently had been optimistic about the future.

O'Fallon moved quickly, searching the first floor, and then crept up the stairs to the second floor. A shot flashed as he opened the first door. He returned the fire as he kicked his way inside. The room was furnished, and Bridger was hiding behind a massive wooden desk.

"My fight's not with you," O'Fallon said. He was standing beside the door. "I want Culver. Get out of my way, maybe I won't kill you."

"Go to hell."

O'Fallon considered his options. He could continue to search the building blindly. He could leave Bridger here to come after him again. He could wait until Bridger was killed, which might take all night, and allow time for more of Culver's men to come to his aid.

Or O'Fallon could come up on Bridger from behind.

Sean shot twice in quick succession and then moved through the door in the adjoining office. He tried the window. The new paint caused it to stick, and then to fly open. O'Fallon holstered his gun and stepped onto the ledge.

A small layer of ice had started to form, but it was not as bad as some of the hill trails he had had to navigate back in Tennessee. His feet felt slippery on the ledge, but his hands easily found crevices in the bricks used in the building. The cold wind bit him, but he did not slow down. He covered the twenty feet in only a few seconds, though it seemed like hours.

The window to the adjoining office was covered with frost. The room had no lights, so O'Fallon could not see where Bridger was waiting. No matter. O'Fallon now had no choice but to gamble. He took a deep breath of the sharp air, grabbed hold of the brick framing the window, and then dived feetfirst through the glass, shielding his face with his arms.

Sean landed on thick carpet in a shower of glass and frozen drizzle. Bridger had moved close to the door, waiting perhaps for O'Fallon to enter from that direction. O'Fallon pulled his Remington, and shot, as Bridger turned and fired his gun. Sean's bullet caught the large man in the neck.

At first, Bridger looked shocked. He placed his hand on

the wound as blood spurted. His face turned pale, and then he fell to the floor.

O'Fallon stepped over the body as he emptied the spent shells from his gun. He went through the door, and felt cool metal at the base of his head before he heard the click of a gun being cocked.

"Well, Mr. O'Fallon. So we meet again." It was the voice of the banker, Braddock. "Don't move, or I'll blow your head off."

Chapter 22

Sean stood quietly, the Remington useless in his hand. The snow entered the window, settled on the floor, melted. The wind howled through the broken glass.

Braddock pulled his gun back several inches from O'Fallon and said, "Move very slowly. Throw your gun over there, out of the way."

O'Fallon did as he was told.

"I knew you were working for Culver," O'Fallon said. "I hated to see you get away. Guess everything kind of evens out in the end."

"I expected to see you tonight, even though nobody else thought it possible. How'd you do it? Are you working for Simpson?"

Braddock seemed much different than the first time they had met. At that time, Braddock had seemed to be a soft, cowardly man. Now, he was quite competent. His voice was strong. The gun in his hand remained pointed steadily at O'Fallon. The wind blew stronger through the window. Sean said, "This is between me and Culver."

"So I'll bring you to Culver. After all this commotion, he'll be expecting you, too."

"So Culver is here?" O'Fallon said.

"Where else would he be? He's with that Indian woman of yours."

O'Fallon felt colder than the wind blowing through the

window. It was worse than any nightmare. How could his worst enemy have Maria? How could O'Fallon have again failed the woman he loved? And how could he have failed himself? He had set the charges, planned to blow up the building . . . but had he done so, he would have also killed Maria.

Braddock watched O'Fallon's face, and grinned. "So you are sweet on the woman, after all? That's interesting. Culver might enjoy having you watch him take your woman . . . repeatedly."

O'Fallon turned slowly, collecting his wits. "This wasn't your fight," he said. "Just like it wasn't Bridger's, or Oxman's. But you've all made it your fight. The only man I really want to kill is Culver. Now, I'll gladly kill you, as well."

"You are a cocky son of a bitch, aren't you?" Braddock waved his gun casually at Bridger. "No matter. I must thank you for disposing of these two fools. It saves me the trouble—"

Suddenly a strong gust of wind blew through the broken window, bringing with it a cloud of snow and wet fog. It was only a small distraction, but it was enough. Sean ducked beneath Braddock's gun. O'Fallon's shoulder hit Braddock in the stomach. He seemed to be pudgy, but the bulk was muscle. O'Fallon lashed out with a quick right, and then a left to the stomach. His fist felt as if it were hitting a solid board covered with cloth. It didn't stop Braddock, but slowed him down.

He shot three times, all of them just inches from where O'Fallon had just been. He grabbed Bridger's gun and returned the fire. Braddock dived behind the desk, where Bridger had hid just a few minutes before. O'Fallon ran into the hallway.

The shots could be heard through the door of Culver's office. Maria frowned. Culver ignored her expression and kept talking as if nothing were out of the ordinary.

"Do you enjoy wine? Here, have a glass! I assure you, it

is as good as any that comes from France." He handed Maria a glass and then took a sip from his own. "You are a very pretty woman, in spite of the hardships of your travel." He wrinkled his nose. "Perhaps you would like to wash up? No, on second thought we don't have that much time. We can . . . talk just as you are."

"We have nothing to talk about."

"No? We could start with how you and your boyfriend got involved in a fight that you can't win. Or we could start with what you know about the land survey conducted in the nation. Or we could attend to pleasure from the very beginning. It is still several hours until morning, and I intend to take advantage of that time. What do you say?"

Maria threw her glass at Culver. It missed, and shattered against the opposite wall. The man laughed and grabbed her arm. More shots sounded. Culver said, "You're spunky. I like that. It's been quite a few years since I've had that kind of fun, and this seems like a good opportunity to catch up." He put down his glass and tenderly stroked Maria's face. "How do you want it the first time? You can make it as easy or as difficult as you want."

"You try it, and I'll kill you."

"No. I think not." Culver laughed. "I'm not easy to kill."

"Sean is here. If I don't kill you first, he will."

"Wrong again. What you say is not possible. I have guards around this building, and my best man is even now investigating. My men have no doubt found some vagrant and are having a bit of fun with him. A different kind of fun, I might add, than I intend to have with you." Culver pulled Maria to him and kissed her neck. She brought her knee up to his groin, but his other hand stopped the movement before it connected. He pushed himself against her, caressing the leg beneath her dress.

Sean considered his next move. His main concern had shifted from finding Culver to finding Maria, though Braddock said they were together. O'Fallon checked the gun in his hand. It was a different caliber than his Remington and

A COLD, DARK TRAIL

had only one shell left in the chamber. Where could he find another weapon?

He remembered Oxman's gun, downstairs. It was empty, but O'Fallon remembered it was the same caliber as his Remington. It would work. He moved toward the stairs. The smell of gun smoke filled the building. O'Fallon made his way by feel through the darkness. He carefully found the top step and started down. The stairs were not steep, but O'Fallon's leg had started to throb. In the previous excitement he had ignored the pain. Now, it could not be ignored.

O'Fallon moved slowly, patiently finding his way toward the floor below.

Suddenly, Braddock was standing at the bottom of the stairs. He was a darker shape against the other shadows. O'Fallon crouched to take aim. He had only one bullet left, and had to make it count. As his legs bent, however, his bum leg gave out on him and he started to roll down the steps. His last bullet went wild, harmlessly hitting the wall near the staircase. Sean instinctively reached out for something to break his fall. His fingers felt metal. He reached out and clutched the gas fixture, which cracked and came out in his hand along with a length of feeder pipe. He felt the sudden, cool hiss of gas, but only for a second as he continued his fall.

O'Fallon formed himself into a ball and tried to take most of the force with his shoulders.

Braddock, surprised, shot several times at where O'Fallon had been. The two men hit with a solid thud that knocked them both to the floor. O'Fallon took advantage of the situation by forcing himself off the floor with his good leg. His head hit Braddock solidly in the solar plexus, knocking the wind out of him.

He hit the bigger man's head with the gun. It was only a glancing blow, but forced him off balance. Anger filled Braddock's face. He aimed his own gun, but O'Fallon had again slipped into the shadows before the next shot could be fired.

Braddock listened to the footsteps. He took a different route to intercept O'Fallon.

Sean knew he was making too much noise, but his leg hurt so much that he didn't care. He retraced the steps to the office where Oxman's body lay, still warm. Blood had covered the floor, filling the room with its sticky smell. O'Fallon found the dead Indian's gun, wiped off the blood as best he could, and quickly reloaded. He finished with the gun just as Braddock rounded a corner.

O'Fallon waited in the door as the larger man approached. Braddock saw him, but did not fire. Only at the last second did Sean hurry back into the room. He used his good leg to jump on one of the chairs, and then to the desk in the center of the room.

Braddock, still angry, ran at a low crouch spraying the room with bullets. His boots hit the blood-slick floor, however, causing the shots to go wild. O'Fallon squeezed the trigger of his gun, but the result was only a quiet click. Braddock's arms waved wildly as he tried to catch his balance, trying to point the gun in O'Fallon's direction.

Sean knelt on the desk, ignoring the pain in his leg, and took careful aim and fired three more shots in rapid succession. This time the response was three satisfying booms. Three holes appeared in the front of Braddock's coat as he slid across the floor, his blood mixing with the dead Indian's.

Still, Braddock lived. He started to lift his gun again, and O'Fallon shot one final time. The impact forced Braddock back and through the window. It was just a short fall, but left bits of bloody flesh on the broken glass. O'Fallon stepped down from the desk and looked out the window. Braddock's blood was already staining the icy ground below.

Sean still had to find Maria.

The gaslight in Culver's office flickered, and almost went out, as if the gas was no longer reaching the fixture. It was only a small thing, and probably insignificant, but the shooting had also stopped. Culver pulled back and pushed Maria into the chair behind her. He still wasn't too concerned. Braddock and the two Indians would surely have taken care of the intruder. Braddock would, of course, give him a brief report. Culver could then return to his pleasure. On the other hand, it never hurt to be cautious.

He poured a glass of wine, smoothed his coat, and sat down in his large leather chair behind the desk. He opened the top drawer a crack, checked to make sure his small revolver was still handy.

Maria was breathing heavily from her struggles, though Culver had just barely started with her. After Braddock's report, Culver planned to take her to his apartment in the building, where he could have a little more privacy and would not have to listen to Braddock cleaning up the mess. Culver preferred to remain aloof from such petty matters.

Chapter 23

The search of the building took only minutes, though it seemed like hours to Sean. He found no more guards. The only movement and sound now seemed to come from one of the lighted offices on the top floor, which the others had kept him from. O'Fallon knew Maria and Culver were behind the closed door under which a sliver of light slipped into the hall. O'Fallon walked softly, listening to Culver's voice. It was deep, resonant, that of a leader or a politician, even muffled through the thick door.

The talking stopped. O'Fallon kicked open the door, sending splinters across the room. He leveled his revolver at Culver and said, "I've waited a long, long time for this moment. Go ahead. Make a move. I'll shoot you right now."

It wasn't the speech he had planned, but at this point it made no difference. The flickering gaslight reminded O'Fallon that time was now a critical factor. He knew blasting powder, but knew little about gas. How much gas in a building would be dangerous? How much time did he have before the torn gas line near the stairs filled the building to explosive levels? It had only been a few minutes—but he was perhaps lucky that the building had not already blown. Even a small explosion would trigger the charges he had set in the basement. He had no time for long speeches. So why didn't he just shoot the other man?

After all the years and all the miles, now that Sean had

finally caught up with his enemy, he did not shoot. He waited, motionless.

Maria said, "Sean! We heard the shooting, and . . . I knew it had to be you." She knew better than to run to O'Fallon and distract him. Too much could still happen.

Culver smiled politely, as if he were being asked a difficult question at a dinner party rather than facing a loaded gun aimed at his belly. He held a glass. An open bottle of wine was on his desk. Culver acted like a man who couldn't be surprised. He said, "So you must be Sean O'Fallon." He took a sip of wine. "Just who the hell are you, anyway?" His voice carried authority.

"I'm the man that's going to kill you," O'Fallon said.

"Oh," Culver said. "Before you do, perhaps we could have another drink?"

This was also not according to plan. In all of his nightmares and all of his dreams, O'Fallon had never envisioned the final meeting to be like this. Culver did not wait for an answer, but started to refill his glass.

"Would you like a glass of wine, Mr. O'Fallon?"

O'Fallon said to Culver, "You shut up for a minute." He then said to Maria, without ever taking his eyes off Culver, "How are you doing?"

"I was treated rough. I'll live. I knew you'd show up."

"I should never have left you in New Hope. Maybe I shouldn't have left you at all." He added, "Your two kidnappers are dead. So is Braddock."

Culver responded smoothly, without hesitation. "I have to thank you for that," he said. "Those two . . . Indians heard I was interested in the Indian Territory. That much is true, for what businessman in this day and age could ignore such large tracts of land? Somehow they got the idea I would resort to violence to obtain information about the territory." His tongue made a clucking sound. "They were so mistaken!"

"You're a liar. I know that Bridger and Oxman were working for Braddock. And Braddock was working for you."

"Yes. Tragic, isn't it? To have this kind of scandal going

on in my organization. I guess I should have kept a closer watch over my subordinates." He sighed. "You try to trust people, and where does it get you?" He took a sip of wine. "I'm glad you were able to bring this mess to my attention. I assure you, I *will* get to the bottom of this."

O'Fallon knew Culver was lying through his teeth. Yet, the man was a smooth one. Since O'Fallon had entered the room, Culver had been calm and rational. In spite of the years of hate, Sean knew he could not kill this man in cold blood, no matter how much he deserved it. Silence filled the room. O'Fallon said, "I ought to go ahead and shoot you."

Culver said, "You've damaged my organization. You've killed my men, and in one case killed an old friend of mine. It's obvious you've come here to kill me. I would like to know, however, why you want to kill me. I don't know you. I have never had anything to do with you. Are you working for Simpson, after all?"

O'Fallon said softly, "Laura."

Culver raised his eyebrows.

"The former Laura Brannigan, the late Mrs. Sean O'Fallon."

Culver said, "Never heard of her."

"Laura O'Fallon. Born 1848. Died 1865. Murdered at the hands of you and your so-called Culver's Raiders. It was during the war. You probably never knew her name, or cared, while you and your men gang-raped and killed her. Our home was a little hill farm in the Cumberlands, back in Tennessee, and I was away at war."

"Your wife? I assure you, I was never in that region." He picked up a glass and the wine bottle. "And I assure you, if I ever had been in that area, I would never have allowed such atrocities to occur." He walked around the desk without fear or hesitation. "I mean nobody any harm. Let me pour you a drink—"

Culver moved fast. He brought the wine bottle against the side of O'Fallon's head, showering him with glass and wine. Blood spurted from the new gash over his ear. The remaining part of the bottle in Culver's hand was sharp and jagged. He slashed at O'Fallon. Sean dodged most of the thrust, but the bottle hit his arm, knocking the gun to the floor. As Sean fell, Culver kicked at O'Fallon's sore leg. He felt the pain shoot through his body.

Culver tossed the remaining part of the wine bottle to one side, stepped over to Maria.

"You're a fool," Culver said. "Did I kill your wife? Probably. It made no difference to me then. It makes no difference to me now." He looked at Maria, then suddenly grabbed her dress and pulled. It ripped in his hand, revealing the woman's skin. "You pushed me too far, Sean O'Fallon. I don't care who you are, but I'm going to make you pay for what you have done to me. I am going to take your woman, and then I am going to kill her, just as I did your wife. And I am going to enjoy every minute of it."

He walked back behind his desk, pulled open the drawer, and lifted out the handgun. It was of small caliber, but would be deadly enough at close range.

"Your leg hurts, does it?" He aimed the gun. "Tell you what I will do. I'll make it a matched set, just in case you get ideas of being a hero while I enjoy your woman. Of course, you won't be a cripple for long. When I get through with her, I'll finish you off, as well. I'm sure those hours will seem long, however, with a shattered kneecap . . ."

O'Fallon could barely see Culver over the top of the desk. He was in great pain, but he could not let Culver win. He could not let Maria down. Suddenly, all the years of hatred that had festered inside O'Fallon broke loose. He yelled, enraged, got his good leg beneath him and his shoulder under the edge of the desk. He yelled again, and moved the heavy oak desk as if it was cardboard. The desk tilted backward, crushing Culver's legs beneath him. Culver shot wildly, but missed as O'Fallon leaped over the desk.

Culver tried to move, but couldn't. His legs were pinned.

Blood dripped in Sean's eyes, but it made no difference. He was already blinded by rage, anger, frustration, hatred. His hands found Culver's neck and squeezed. O'Fallon's hands were like bands of steel tightening around the smooth skin of Culver's neck.

Culver's jugular throbbed softly under his thumbs. O'Fallon squeezed tighter. The tougher bands of muscle rippled under his fingers, until they started to spasm under the relentless pressure. Culver's breathing grew more shallow. His face became more red. His eyes started to bulge.

Still, O'Fallon did not let go, but started to pound the former guerrilla leader's head against the floor. The head bounced up and down. The sound echoed through the room. O'Fallon continued the pressure on the sensitive windpipe. Culver's face turned purple, and the body finally grew limp.

Only then did O'Fallon's vision start to return. The darkness started to clear from his eyes. He shook his head to rid the blood from his eyes. The body of Culver lay unmoving under him. His hands were still wrapped strongly around the outlaw's throat.

Maria said, "Sean." She touched him on the shoulder. "Sean. Look at me. He's dead. Let him go."

O'Fallon threw the head to the floor one final time, and stood painfully. He wiped the blood from his face, noticed Maria's torn dress. He removed his coat and wrapped it around her. He said, "We've got to get out of here. There's a gas leak downstairs. It could blow at any time. I have a wagon down the street. Our best bet is to get to the horses and get as far away as possible."

He picked up the gun, glanced at Culver, took Maria's hand. O'Fallon thought he saw an impossible flicker of movement in Culver's hand. He thought about one final shot to the head, but there was too much gas in the building. Now, O'Fallon and Maria had to reach safety. The two rushed down the hall and out the front door. Maria followed Sean's lead toward the rear of the building. They had rounded the corner when a figure suddenly pulled himself up to the window ledge of Culver's office.

Maria pointed and said, "Sean! It's Culver! He was dead! How could he—"

Culver broke the window with his gun, aimed it at O'Fallon, who grabbed Maria and dived, covering her body with his.

The former guerrilla leader shot once. The orange flash from the gun ignited a larger flash, which set his clothes on fire. He fell from the window. A huge fireball blew out all the first-story windows. Flames shot back through the empty windowframes, followed by four dull explosions from the basement area.

The walls caved in on themselves. The brick shattered. The wood framework added fuel to the fire. In minutes, the entire crumbled building was in flames.

Chapter 24

Flames shot into the cold, wet night air. The collapsed walls of the Culver Building, engulfed by flames and dust, created steam which mixed with the snow and fog and icy rain. O'Fallon felt drained. In the distance, a fire siren sounded. He leaned his back against the wall and slid down it slowly, oblivious to the icy cold. Culver was dead, and that was all that mattered. Nobody could have escaped the inferno.

O'Fallon watched the orange glow of the fire, felt its heat on his face. He closed his eyes, heard the clang of the approaching fire engines.

He felt very tired. The cuts to his head were not serious, but were starting to hurt. The cold and dampness seeped through his pants, causing his leg to throb.

"Thank goodness it's over," he said to Maria. "Maybe we can get some peace."

Maria didn't answer.

"Maria?"

O'Fallon opened his eyes. He froze as the firelight glinted off the knife held at Maria's throat. He slowly started to stand.

"That's it, O'Fallon," Culver said. "Move real slow. One wrong move and your woman is dead."

It was the first and last time that O'Fallon had ever seen Maria scared. She had a slightly crazed look in her eyes, as the cold blade touched her neck. Sean understood. She had been through so much over the past several weeks, months, years. O'Fallon felt responsible for part of it; he had never intended her to become involved, yet her life was again in danger.

Culver, however, looked even more crazed. He had just seen his dreams go up in an explosion. He no longer had a future. His hair was tangled. His face was blackened and burned. His lips were dry and puffy. His clothes hung on him in tatters. Blood was seeping from his mouth, nose, and ears. How could the man have survived the explosion? How could he still live, much less be strong enough to hold Maria? It seemed impossible.

O'Fallon had lost the Remington in the explosion, but he was still holding the dead Indian's gun. He moved it upward, slightly, but a sudden tensing of muscles in Culver's forearms caused O'Fallon to lower his hand again. He was fast, but he would not be able to shoot before Culver could push the knife into Maria's soft flesh.

"Smart move, hillbilly. Just stay smart, if you want your woman to live."

The horse-drawn fire equipment and the firemen had arrived and were spraying the surrounding buildings to keep the fire from spreading. O'Fallon, Maria, and Culver were in a secluded alley, hidden from the crowds that had suddenly materialized in response to the fire.

"All right," Culver said. "Now. O'Fallon, throw your gun over there, against that retaining wall."

Sean obeyed. The alley was puddled with icy water. The gun made a splash as it hit. Culver smiled. The sleet and rain running off the man's burned face gave him a demonic look.

"Back up against that building."

O'Fallon followed the order. The wall was cold against his back. He considered his next move.

"Sean . . ." Maria's voice was a croak as she struggled for control. "Don't . . . mind me. Kill him." She tried to spit, but her mouth was dry. Culver's hold on her throat was too restrictive. He tightened his grip even more, cutting off her breath.

Then suddenly, Maria kicked, awkwardly but solidly. Culver pressed down on the knife, but Maria had twisted and the blade mainly hit the leather collar of O'Fallon's heavy coat that he had wrapped around her. O'Fallon moved in, grabbed Culver's arm that held the knife, twisted it away from Maria's neck. Culver loosened his grip, and Maria fell to the ground, clutching her throat and a tiny streak of red that had not been protected by the coat.

Culver was still surprisingly strong. The hand holding the knife inched toward Sean, who hit Culver in the mouth. Blood droplets sprayed from the mouth, but he did not let up his steady pressure. Culver shifted, and suddenly, unexpectedly, was free. He was standing and facing O'Fallon. It was a good move—a wrestling move.

The two men came together again. Both were strong fighters, but had been weakened. Neither gained an advantage over the other for long minutes. Culver slipped on the wet ground. As he went down, however, he kicked out. Culver's foot hit with unerring accuracy. New pain shot through O'Fallon's leg and side, and this time he screamed.

Culver followed the move with a blow to O'Fallon's bleeding head.

Sean gasped. Culver laughed. O'Fallon, however, had lived with much worse pain for many years. He clamped his mouth shut as Culver moved in warily, knife in hand. O'Fallon rested on the ground, breathing heavily, allowing Culver to come closer.

Suddenly, O'Fallon dived and rolled. The pain in his leg was terrible, but he was not going to let Culver live, not now. His body hit Culver, crashing him against the stone wall.

O'Fallon then had the other man's arm twisted behind his back, heard a satisfying crack as it bent backward. He took Culver's head, already tender and bruised from the fight inside the building, and crashed it against the stones.

The blow would have stunned most men, but Culver managed to push O'Fallon away and dive behind some crates stacked near the wall.

O'Fallon picked up the knife. This time he was the one

doing the stalking. He cautiously moved along the wall, illuminated by the fire at the former Culver Building. His shirt was rapidly becoming stiff with frozen rain and blood. His arms were becoming numb. Still, he moved on, searching among the debris for his enemy.

He heard a rustle, but did not shoot at the burned paper falling from the sky. It hit the ground, sizzled, and grew soggy.

O'Fallon kicked a box to one side.

Nothing.

O'Fallon took another step, using the wall to steady himself. He was getting weaker. His head was spinning. The alley grew darker, and quieter.

Suddenly, he felt a presence. It was the same feeling he had in Tennessee when he knew instinctively a snake was in the woodpile, waiting to strike. He had a feeling of being watched, of a shadow near him. He fell to the ground, just as Culver leaped at him from the top of the wall.

As he turned, his back to the ground, O'Fallon lifted the bone-handled knife.

Culver's eyes bulged as he landed. The knife buried itself up to its handle in Culver's chest. Blood spurted from the new wound. Culver's hands clutched one final time at Sean before his body finally went limp.

Breathing heavily, O'Fallon rolled Culver's body into a frozen puddle, the knife sticking out from his heart.

This time Sean stepped over to the body, checked the flaccid wrist for a pulse to make sure Culver was dead. Only then did he turn his back on Culver and walk to where he had left Maria. She was calm. She met him as he approached. Now, the rain, ice, sleet, and snow were coming down hard. O'Fallon's leg gave out from under him, and he fell to the ground.

Maria kneeled beside him.

"Sean?"

"It's all right. It's over. Finally. It's over."

Sean stood with Maria's help and walked to the edge of the alley. The fire was burning down.

"And what about you, Sean O'Fallon? What is your next move? Back to Tennessee?"

The voice was questioning, urging, but not pushing. She was waiting, hoping.

"No. I can't go back. There are too many painful memories. Tennessee is no longer my home. It can never be my home again." The crowd watching the fire had grown, and was now almost to the alley. He looked at Maria. "This is a hell of a time, but I think what we shared gives us both certain privileges. I love you, Maria. Whatever I do now, I want to do it with you. My home now is with you, wherever you are. If you will have me."

Her kiss was the answer both had been searching for.

About the Author

Frank Watson is a journalist who lives in Missouri.